WOULD YOU BE INTERESTED IN TRAVELING THROUGH A PORTAL IN TIME?

The Personal Adventures of Time Travelers

Earle W. Hanna Sr.

iUniverse, Inc.
Bloomington

Would You Be Interested in Traveling through a Portal in Time?
The Personal Adventures of Time Travelers

iUniverse books may be ordered through booksellers or by contacting:

iUniverse
1663 Liberty Drive
Bloomington, IN 47403
www.iuniverse.com
1-800-Authors (1-800-288-4677)

ISBN: 978-1-4620-0706-6 (sc)
ISBN: 978-1-4620-0708-0 (e)
ISBN: 978-1-4620-0707-3 (hc)

Printed in the United States of America

iUniverse rev. date: 10/4/2011

CONTENTS

THE GYROSCOPE

My name is George Mac Dowel, and my wife, Linda, and I like to go to flea markets. Linda looks for antiques to buy at bargain prices, and I look for parts to use in my projects. One day while browsing around the tables in one of our favorite outdoor flea markets, I found a very small gyroscope. It was smaller than a walnut and appeared to have little pieces of crystal embedded in the wheel. The gyroscope seemed to be making a very faint humming noise. When I picked it up, I could feel it vibrating. As I held it, I felt a warm sensation traveling through my hand and up my arm. It seemed to be trying to communicate with me. I suddenly felt as if I had to have the gyroscope. I wanted to buy it.

The little old man that owned the items displayed on the table was sitting in a beat-up old rocking chair under a tree a few feet away. I held up the gyroscope and asked, "How much do you want for this?"

"Two bucks," he answered.

Is this thing really worth two dollars? I was ready to put it back on the table when I felt the warm sensation traveling up my arm again, and then the gyroscope started to vibrate and make a loud humming noise. I could hear it distinctly humming, "Buy me. Buy me." I was wondering whether the old man could hear the noise that it was making.

He apparently didn't because, thinking that I was going to put it back on the table, he said, "You look like a man who is handy and can fix things so I'll even throw in this bag of small parts." He picked up an old, dusty canvas bag that looked as if it had been in storage for years. "That thing you have in your hand was in this bag. This bag of parts came from the estate of a man who told everyone in his family that he was abducted by aliens from outer space and that they had given him all kinds of gifts." Laughing loudly, he said, "You never know, you may be purchasing a bag full of their gifts."

Without any hesitation, I put my hand in my pocket, pulled out my wallet, and handed him two dollars. He smiled, handed me the bag, and said, "Good luck, son. I hope you can use that stuff."

I said thank you, put the gyroscope in the bag with the other parts, and went on my way through the maze of tables to look for my wife. As I was walking, I could feel vibrations and hear the humming coming from the bag. It sounded as if the gyroscope was speaking to me. "Build something with me. Build something with me." Exactly what it wanted me to build, I didn't know, but I felt a burning desire to find Linda, return to my shop, and make something with the gyroscope as soon as possible.

I found her at one of the tables looking at some old furniture. I asked her if she didn't mind if we went home. She replied, "We may as well leave. I haven't found anything that I like. What is in that dirty old bag, George?"

"Just some parts that I can use in one of my projects that I'm really excited about," I answered. I like to think that I am an inventor, and I wanted to build something—even though nothing that I have built has ever worked.

When we arrived at our home in northeast Philadelphia, I immediately took the bag to my shop at the rear of our garage. I could feel the gyroscope vibrating in the bag and making humming noises as if it was trying to speak again.

I emptied the bag on my workbench, picked the gyroscope out of the pile of parts, and laid it at the far side of the bench. It was humming louder, and it sounded as if it was saying, "Put my cube next to me—I want you to build something." I searched through the pile of parts and found what appeared to be a brass cube slightly smaller than the gyroscope. The gyroscope was on its side, but as soon as I placed the cube next to it, it stood up on end and the wheel started to spin.

I moved back from my workbench and said, "I have to be hallucinating—this junk can't move and talk."

As the gyroscope's wheel was spinning, the humming noise became louder, and it said, "Put us in the box—you can build something."

If these parts were left here by aliens, maybe this gyroscope can communicate and wants me to make something that could be important to people here on earth.

I started digging through the pile of parts and found a box that looked as if it was made of some sort of steel. It was approximately an inch and a half wide, an inch and a half high, and three inches long. On the lid was a speedometer-type dial with little wheels that could be set to date, hour, and minute. On the side of the box was a square metal on and off switch and the lid was sealed shut with small removable metal clips.

I removed the clips, opened the box, and found two sets of small brackets fixed to the inside. When I placed the gyroscope in the larger bracket and the cube in the smaller bracket, the gyroscope started to hum and glow. The humming noise seemed to be saying, "Close the lid and put the switch in the on position, and set the dials to wherever you want to go. I am a time-transporting device that you can hold in your hand! You can only go backward in time and return safely home whenever you want to leave the past. I do not work for traveling in the future—it is forbidden! If you use me, do not loose me or you can never return home!" That was the very last time that the gyroscope ever made any verbal humming sounds that I could understand.

I nervously put the switch in the off position and sealed the lid with the removable metal clips. I heard a slight hum and the dials on the device automatically set to the exact day, date, and time: Saturday, June 20, 2009, 4:06 p.m.

I was extremely curious and I needed to know whether this device could really transport me in time to wherever I wanted to go. I was anxious to test it, but wondered where could I test it and where would I go. I remembered that my house had been one of the last homes built in this development four years earlier. I decided to go back five years and see the houses being constructed. I knew that there was a large vacant lot surrounded by trees near the railroad not far from my house and I could test the device there without being seen.

I put the device in my right pocket. Since I needed something for an excuse to leave the house, I put a few nuts and bolts in a small plastic bag. I slipped the bag over my wallet in my left pocket.

Linda was preparing dinner in the kitchen. I told her that I had to go to the hardware store to pick up some nuts and bolts for my project. Linda said, "Don't be late, George. Dinner will be ready in about an hour."

I replied, "Don't worry. It won't take very long. I'll be back in plenty of time." At least I was hoping that I would return quickly. If I were to get stuck in the past, I knew that I would sure look a little older when I returned.

I went out to my driveway, got into my car, and drove to the vacant lot even though it was only three blocks away from our house. I didn't want Linda to know what I was doing and I had to make it look good.

I parked across from the tree-surrounded lot and walked on the dirt pathway into the open area. I was now ready to test the device. It was 4:21 p.m. and I only wanted to move the last number on the year dial, so I put the switch in the on position. I turned the dial backward from 9 to 8, 7, 6, 5, and 4. As I turned the dial, the gyroscope made a slight humming noise. It took only about five seconds to change the setting to 2004, and it was still 4:21 p.m. I looked at my wristwatch and it was 4:21 p.m. *Did I really travel backward in time? I don't feel anything. Maybe the time-transporting device doesn't work.*

I pushed the switch into the off position and put the device in my pocket. Since nothing seemed to be happening, I decided to go home. I walked back to the street, but my car was gone! When I looked toward my development, I could see that some of the houses were missing. I knew then that I had traveled five years into the past.

Since I was curious to see how the development looked before all of the houses were finished, I walked down the street. When I got to the place where my house should have been, I was looking at a pile of freshly bulldozed dirt. Some of the area was bulldozed flat and ready for construction while some of the houses were partially constructed. It seemed very quiet and I couldn't figure out why no one was working on the houses on a Saturday. Usually the builders worked at least six days a week and took off Sunday.

There was a lady walking her dog at the far end of the development and I really wanted to talk to someone, but she turned and started walking in the opposite direction. I decided not to search for anyone to speak to because I was getting a little worried about being able to return home. I went back to the lot, hoping that I wouldn't have any problems.

I pulled the device from my pocket. I wanted to return home at 4:45 p.m., so that I would not be late for dinner. When I looked at the dials to reset them to return home, they read: Sunday, June 20, 2004, 5:03 p.m.! I said, "Oh no! Something is wrong with the device. I left home on Saturday." Frantically I turned the switch on and reset the dials to Saturday, June 20, 2009, 4:45 p.m., and the gyroscope hummed again.

Once again, nothing seemed to happen and I was hoping that I had returned home. I turned off the switch, put the device in my pocket, and started walking to where I had parked my car. When I saw the car, I shouted, "Halleluiah! I made it home!"

As I drove home, I wondered why the dial was set to Sunday, June 20, when I was ready to return home. The device seemed to work perfectly. That's it! I know why the dial was set to Sunday—the days of the month fall on different dates each year. June 20, 2004, must have fallen on a Sunday. The device works perfectly—it sets the days automatically.

When I got home, Linda was almost ready to set out dinner. She asked, "Did you get the parts that you needed?"

"Yes." I pulled the small bag from my pocket. "I'll be right back. I'm going to put them on my workbench."

I went into my shop, put the bag on my bench and the device in my drawer, and returned to the kitchen to have dinner with Linda.

I wanted to tell her about the device, but I thought that I should take one more trip into the past to make sure that I could work it properly. She might want to travel back in time with me and I had to make sure that I did not put her in any danger.

That evening, I wasn't able to fall asleep for a long time. I kept thinking about where I would like to travel. Then it came to me. My grandfather had told me that he met my grandmother while he was having coffee in a restaurant at the corner of Second and Market Streets in Philadelphia in June 1930. She was the most beautiful waitress that he had ever seen. From that moment on, he knew that she was the woman that he wanted to marry. I decided that I would go to the restaurant on Sunday morning and have a cup of coffee.

Linda and I had already made plans to go to the movies and dinner on Sunday, but I would leave on my adventure and return home with time to spare no matter how long I stayed in 1930.

The device was still keeping perfect time when I took it out of the drawer. The dial read Sunday, June 21, 2009, 8:56 a.m.

I told Linda that I had to go out for a little while and that I would return in two or three hours. I knew that I would have to spend some money, so I stopped at the coin store in the mall to buy some inexpensive coins and currency that had been used in the 1920s.

After I bought the coins and currency, I drove to Oxford Circle near Roosevelt Boulevard and parked the car. I knew that the area of the northeast that I lived in would be a long distance from the developed area of the city in 1930, and I didn't want to walk very far to find public transportation.

After getting out of the car, I walked up a driveway behind a row of houses and turned on my time-transporting device. It was 10:26 a.m. when I turned the dials slowly back to June 21, 1930. I decided to move the dials slowly so that I could control the spot where I was going to stop. It was possible to become a permanent part of a tree or a building when I stopped at my final destination—and I wanted to be able to move to a safe area as I was being transported.

When I turned the switch off, I was standing in a wooded area near some newly constructed homes. I put the device in my pocket, walked out of the woods onto a paved street, and headed toward Roosevelt Boulevard.

An older gentleman on the corner was reading a newspaper. Since I wanted to go to Center City, I thought that he might be able to give me directions. I walked up and asked, "Sir, how can I get to Center City Philadelphia?"

He answered, "Are you from Texas, son?"

I guess that was because I was wearing a short-sleeved chambray shirt and tight jeans. I answered, "No, I'm actually from up north."

He looked puzzled. He nodded his head as if he was agreeing with me and probably thinking that I was a little odd. Then he said, "Take the trolley car—it's about two blocks straight down that street in front of you—and then transfer to the elevated train at Bridge Street. The train will take you to Center City."

I replied, "Thank you, sir, for the information," and went on my way.

As I was walking to the trolley stop, I was totally amazed to see the antique Ford, Chevrolet, and Packard automobiles that were passing me by on the streets. *Those aren't antiques; I'm looking at the real thing!* I had to watch my step on the cobblestone streets, because there were a few horse-drawn wagons leaving horse manure on the streets.

I really wanted to have a cup of coffee in the restaurant where my grandfather met my grandmother. Maybe I would see one of them in there. I had seen so many of their pictures in an old album that I know exactly how they looked when they were young.

It seemed as if it was taking forever for the trolley car to arrive. When the trolley car finally stopped, the conductor pushed a lever to open the folding doors and I got on. I told the conductor that I wanted to go to Center City Philadelphia and return by the same route. He said that I should buy two tokens for ten cents, and that he would give me a transfer for one of the tokens, which would get me on the elevated train. I gave him a dime and he gave me one token in change and one transfer slip. I walked past some of the other passengers to the middle of the trolley car and sat on one of the wooden benches.

The trolley car creaked and rocked from side to side as we traveled to the end of the line. This was becoming an exciting journey and I wasn't even to my final destination. After several stops, I got off with the remaining passengers and started walking to the elevated train station, which was close by. I walked up the steps to the tollbooth and I handed the man my transfer, pushed the wooden turnstile aside, walked to the platform, and waited for the train.

The platform wasn't very crowded. When the train stopped, the doors opened and I got on. Padded benches were fastened to the walls the length of car and covered with woven yellow wicker. There were only a few people on the train so I had my choice of seats. I sat and waited with anticipation for my stop.

The train swayed as it sped along the tracks. When we reached Fairmount Avenue, it went down into the underground tunnel the same as it does in my own time period. When I got off at Second and Market Streets, I was so excited that I raced up the steps to the restaurant.

I had seen this restaurant, which is still standing in my own time period, but it was so different looking at it in 1930. I couldn't wait to go inside so I hurried across the street and sat on a stool at the counter.

The old round spinning stools with the red leather seats were impressive, but the gray marble counter top was even more impressive. A short thin man wearing a white hat cooked eggs on the grill. When he saw me, he said, "The waitress will be with you soon—she's in the kitchen." I noticed a few people in the wooden booths near the windows. Then the waitress came walking out of the kitchen at the far end of the restaurant. She set a plate with a sandwich on it in front of the man at the other end of the counter, walked over to me, and said, "What can I get for you, sir?"

I was looking into the eyes of my own grandmother—the future Mrs. Mary Mac Dowel! She was young and beautiful—just like in her wedding pictures. She was tall and thin with long brown hair and beautiful brown eyes. For a moment, I was speechless. She stared at me and then I said, "I'll have a cup of coffee."

She was still staring at me and then she said, "You look very familiar—have we ever met before?"

I almost slipped when I answered, "Not yet. I'm sorry—I mean—no we haven't."

She smiled at my foolish answer and said, "You have a strange resemblance to a man that I have dated a couple of times. Do you have a brother by the name of Lester Mac Dowel?"

"No, I don't," I answered.

I started to feel uncomfortable knowing that I was talking to my future grandmother about my future grandfather when she said, "You are really a good looking guy. I'll bet all the girls tell you that."

"No, they don't. I haven't really been dating lately."

"Well I wouldn't mind going out with you, handsome." Then she walked over to the coffee urn to pour me a cup.

As she was pouring the coffee, I thought, *I have to get out of here! I think my own grandmother is trying to pick me up.*

After she put the cup of coffee in front of me, I said nervously, "I'm married."

"That's too bad," she replied. "Would you like anything else?"

"No, I'm in a hurry. I have an appointment."

"That will be five cents, handsome."

I took a dime out of my pocket, handed it to her, and said, "Keep the change."

"Thank you. Come back anytime." She walked over to a customer that had just come in and was seated in a booth near the window. As she was taking his order, I put sugar in my coffee and drank it as fast as I could. When she went into the kitchen, I got up and almost ran out of the restaurant.

I started walking at a fast pace for a few blocks west on Market Street in the direction of city hall. As I was walking, I thought that I should not have gone to the restaurant. It was wrong to be talking to my future grandmother. What if my grandfather found out that she was trying to pick up another man? Could something change in the future? I have to make sure that when I travel back in time that I don't ever visit any of my relatives in the past.

I was calming down by the time I reached the corner of Eight and Market Streets and stopped in front of Gimbels Department Store. I knew that this had always been the main shopping district of Philadelphia, and the center of activity, but the sidewalks didn't seem much crowed with people.

I started looking in Gimbels display windows at the clothing that the manikins were wearing and thinking how the styles had really changed over the years. I was curious to see what kind of furniture the average person bought in 1930, so I decided to go in and browse.

I went upstairs on the wooden escalator to the furniture department. As I was looking at the furniture and lamps, I realized that I was looking at things that would be antiques in my time period—and they were brand-new items. The prices were a fraction of what we would pay for them. *What if I could buy some of these things and transport them to the future? We could have some nice antiques in our home. I'll bet they would be some great conversation pieces when we entertain our friends.*

I'd have to tell Linda about this when I get back home. She would never believe that I can travel back in time. I didn't think that it would take much to convince her. I'd just bring her along for the best trip that she has ever taken.

I left the store and decided to walk around the neighborhood. I walked east, looking in all of the shop windows. When I looked into furniture store windows, all that I could see were some great buys. I turned the corner at Third Street and proceeded walking north.

As I was walking, I noticed that the people looked very poor. There were men and women with little children standing in soup lines, just trying to get a hot meal for their families. Then I realized that this was during the Great Depression. People were out of work and just trying to survive. They looked at me as if their situation was hopeless. I felt sorry for them and wanted to tell them that things would get better in the future, but I knew that I couldn't say anything. They wouldn't believe me anyway. I turned around and walked back to Second and Market Streets, and went down the steps to catch the train for my trip home.

When I returned to the wooded area in Oxford Circle section, it was 4:22 p.m. I slowly turned the dials to June 21, 2009, 11:30 a.m., and returned to my own time. I was back in the driveway behind the houses where I had started. I got in my car and drove straight home. I was excited about breaking the news to Linda that I could travel backward in time with something that I had made, but I decided to wait until the next morning to give her a real demonstration.

When I returned home, Linda was making sandwiches for lunch. I said, "I have a surprise for you. You may not believe this, but something that I have made in my shop really works."

"Let me see it, George! What did you invent and what can you do with it?"

"You have to wait until tomorrow morning because I have to take you to a special place to demonstrate it. Let's just keep our plans to see a movie and have dinner today. You can find out all about my invention tomorrow morning."

"Why do you need a special place to demonstrate it?"

"It seems to work better at a different location. There are a lot of stores in the area where I am going to do the demonstration, and you can go shopping when I am finished."

When I mentioned shopping, it seemed to interest Linda more than my invention, because she just loved to shop—even if she wasn't going to buy anything—so she agreed.

I was glad that she had agreed to wait because it had been a long day—and it wasn't over yet. I didn't want to travel into the past right away because I thought that if I became fatigued, I could make a mistake when using the device and put us in danger.

When we got out of bed on Monday morning, Linda said, "George, we forgot that you have to work today!"

"It will be all right. I'm taking a vacation day and I will call the office before we leave."

After breakfast, I called my office and left a message that I would be in on Tuesday. Linda and I were on our way by 8:45.

I parked on a quiet street next to an old factory just off Delaware Avenue in Penn's Landing.

Linda asked, "Why are we stopping here? I don't see any stores."

I told her about my invention and my adventure. After hearing my story, she asked, "Is this a joke, George? You have some kind of a surprise planned for me, don't you?"

"Please believe me. I have been telling you the truth. Let me show you that this time-transporting device really works. I just want to do a little demonstration with it. If you still don't believe me, we'll go home and never talk about it again."

"All right, George. I will humor you, but if this time-transporting device of yours doesn't work, I want you to promise me that you will see a doctor as soon as we get home."

"You have my word. You can even pick the doctor and go with me to his office."

"Let's get your gadget working," she said with a great deal of skepticism.

I got out of the car, walked around to the passenger side, and opened the door. Taking Linda by the hand, I said, "Come with me. I'm going to prove to you that my invention works and that I am not having a mental breakdown."

I had Linda stand on the pavement facing me and then I said, "Hold on to me tightly, my love. I don't want to take the chance of losing you. Wrap your arms around me tightly."

As I turned on the device, she whispered, "I hope there isn't anyone watching us—this really looks silly."

I slowly turned the dials to June 22, 1930. As we were about to stop, I could see that the day coming up on the dial was Sunday. I knew that all Philadelphia stores would be closed because of the state blue laws. Since it would not be a good day for Linda to shop, I moved the dials to Monday, June 23. When I shut off the device, it didn't look like we had moved. We were in front of the same factory. I faced the spot where I had parked the car only a few feet away, but it had vanished.

"Well, when do we start traveling in time, George?"

"Turn around and look at the car."

She turned around and asked, "Where is our car?"

"It's still in the same spot. But we won't be able to see it until we return home. We have arrived at our destination: June 23, 1930."

"You're kidding!"

I held her hand as we walked to Delaware Avenue. We were walking on a red brick pavement next to a cobblestone street when she said, "I can't believe what I am seeing, George. Look at those old automobiles getting on that ferry to cross the Delaware River to Camden, New Jersey. I have only seen Fords and Chevrolets like that in the movies and old magazines. Look at the piers where cargo is being unloaded from the ships onto those old trucks. That is where Penn's Landing should be.

"This is fantastic—you really did it! It's hard to believe that we are actually in 1930. George, your invention can make us rich. We can charge people to take them on trips with your device."

"No, we can't," I replied.

"Why not?"

"Because they will tell their friends and some unscrupulous

person may steal the device. We can't even sell it. Suppose that we sell the device to someone and they decide to travel in the past—and they change the future to suit their own greedy purposes. What would happen to the world as we know it and what would happen to us? It's too dangerous. The gyroscope that operates my time-transporting device is probably the only one in the world—and we are the only ones that can use it. We can't even tell our friends about it."

"I guess that you're right. I never really thought about the consequences."

"I had given some thought to playing the stock market and betting on sports and horse races because we would know the winners in advance."

"That would be dishonest," she said.

"I know. You and I don't believe in cheating anyone and I can't think of any honest way to make money with this device."

We turned west on Market Street. When we reached Second and Market Streets Linda said, "Look, there's a restaurant on the corner. Let's go in and have a cup of coffee and discuss different ideas that we can come up with to make a profit with the device."

"Don't even think about going in there!"

"Why can't we go in the restaurant?"

I took her by the arm and started walking up Market Street. "I was in the restaurant yesterday and my future grandmother is the waitress. She was interested in going out on a date with me until I told her that I was married."

Linda started laughing and said, "That is funny."

"It wasn't funny when I was talking to her. I couldn't wait to get out of there. If I said something wrong, I could have changed my own history. She might have lost interest in my grandfather and I wouldn't exist. I am so glad that nothing had changed when I returned home to you."

"That is scary. We are going to have to be very careful who we meet and talk to when we travel into the past."

"Yes, I know. If we meet anyone that is remotely related to us, we must be on guard and get away from them."

As we passed some furniture stores, Linda said, "Look, George, I have an idea. I know how we can make some money on your invention. We can buy furniture and sell it for a profit in our own time period. Do you think that we can transport furniture to the future with us?"

"I had given that some thought when I was here before, but I didn't plan on selling the furniture. I really thought that it would be nice to have some antique furniture in our home."

She said, "We can buy furniture for our home later. Right now I think that we should make a profit from your device."

"That's a good idea and it's honest. Let's try it. I have some 1920s money that I brought with me."

We went into a store on Market Street and purchased a beautiful small marble-top table. The salesman asked us whether we would like to have it delivered. Linda told him that our car was nearby and that we could carry it.

We carried the table back to the factory on the little street just off of Delaware Avenue. Linda wrapped her right arm around my waist and held the edge of the table with her left hand. I turned on the device and moved the dials very slowly and cautiously forward to the future. It was working! We moved ahead in time with the table. When I shut off the device, we were next to our car. We put the table in the trunk and drove home completely satisfied with our purchase.

When we arrived home, Linda said, "George, we could travel into the past and see history in the making. If we buy antiques in the past and sell them in our own time, we would be able to finance our trips. We could have some really great vacations and stay as long as we want—always returning home on time."

"We could try," I replied. "I don't know how much money we could make because we will need a lot of money from the time period where we purchase the furniture. That could turn out to be quite expensive. We would have to sell the furniture to antique dealers, and then exchange the money that we make at coin dealers."

"We could do it," she said. "It would be exciting just to shop in the past. What about traveling in the future? Have you tried traveling in the future?"

"No. I told you about the gyroscope speaking in those humming sounds—it said that it would not travel into the future. It was forbidden."

"I wonder why."

"I have no idea. It could be dangerous and maybe we wouldn't be able to return home. I wouldn't even think of trying. I'm satisfied with just being able to travel into the past."

We decided to travel back in time the next weekend. During the week, we would sell the table that we had purchased. On Wednesday after work, I picked up Linda and we took the table to an antique dealer. He was amazed at the mint condition of the table and gave us a good price for it. Linda told him that we might be able to find some other pieces that were in the same condition. He said that he would be interested in purchasing them. Anytime that we had furniture or lamps, we should stop in his store.

On Thursday evening, I went to the coin dealer and exchanged our profits for money from the 1920s. The dealer was interested in why I was buying so much old money, since it was all from the late 1920s. I told him that I was buying it for a friend that traveled to Europe quite frequently, and had a market for it. He thanked me for the sale and told me to come back again.

Friday started the long Fourth of July weekend. Linda wanted to stay in 1930 for the entire weekend. I told her that we could stay for the entire week.

"Is that possible, George?"

"Yes," I answered. "We just set the date that we want to arrive at our destination. We can spend a week if you want in 1930 and then return home to see our own Fourth of July celebration."

We packed our suitcases with clothing that looked like things that people wore in the 1930s, and on Saturday morning we were on our way.

We parked the car near the old factory and I unloaded the suitcases from the trunk. Linda held her suitcase in one hand and I put mine between my legs. As Linda held onto my arm, I showed her how to operate the time-transporting device by slowly moving the dials to June 30, 1930, just in case there was an emergency, and we were on our way.

We registered at a local hotel just off Market Street. After we checked in, we decided to walk around the area to see what was happening. The first place on our walking tour was Independence Hall.

At Independence Hall, some politicians were giving speeches from a platform. They were talking about how they were going to create more work for the unemployed. After a while we became bored with their speeches, so we walked up to Rittenhouse Square. A brass band was playing and it was much more entertaining, so we sat on a bench and enjoyed the music.

At around five o'clock, we decided to have dinner at a local restaurant. The food was great and the prices were unbeatable.

After dinner, we decided to check out the nightlife. As we were walking along Chestnut Street, we heard music coming from one of the buildings. We stopped and looked in the open door. Linda said, "Look, it's a dance hall. The dancing looks different than we are used to, but I think we can do it. Let's give it a try. The sign on the window says it will only cost us ten cents each to get in the door."

"It sounds like a good idea and we have nothing else to do this evening," I replied. I paid the man at the door. We went in and, following the moves of the other patrons, started dancing.

We had been dancing and enjoying ourselves for about twenty minutes when Linda said, "Let's take a break and sit at one of those empty tables in the corner."

"I wouldn't mind sitting down for a little while. We've been walking all day."

As we were walking to the table, I said, "Look. Just about everyone in this place is drinking coffee. They must really have some great coffee in this dance hall."

As soon as we sat down, a waiter walked over to our table and asked, "Would you like a cup of something to drink? We have various blends."

Linda said, "I don't really like strong coffee so I'll have something weak."

I said, "Make mine a little stronger and could we have some cream on the side please?"

The waiter broke into a smile and I thought that he was going to burst out laughing when he said, "Certainly, sir."

A few minutes later, he walked back to our table and put our cups in front of us with a small pitcher of cream and said, "That will be seventy five cents each."

I gave him two dollars and said, "Keep the change."

He said, "Thank you, sir."

I said, "This coffee is expensive. I hope it tastes good."

Linda replied, "This doesn't smell like coffee."

I said, "Let's take a sip before we put any cream in it,"

Each of us took a sip at the same time. Linda put her cup down and said, "This isn't coffee! It tastes like some kind of alcohol."

"Mine tastes like some kind of strong gin. I think we are in one of those places that they used to call a speakeasy where they served illegal alcohol."

"You're right," she said. "Prohibition didn't end until 1933."

I said, "I think that we should leave this place. You never know—the police could raid it, and we don't want to be put in jail. We could lose the device and never be able to return home."

"Let's go," replied Linda.

As we were getting up to leave, a fight broke out between two young men. They were fighting over a girl. Some of their friends tried to break it up, and suddenly it became a free for all.

I grabbed Linda's hand and said, "Let's get out of here!" As we were rushing toward the front door, some men and women that were fighting blocked our exit. I pulled the time-transporting device from my pocket and started to set it ahead to the next day. Just as I was moving the dials, I was knocked to the floor and lost my grip on Linda's hand.

When I got to my feet, the room was in darkness. I shouted, "Linda, where are you?" There was no answer and I started to panic. It was almost pitch black in the dance hall so I moved the dials on the device by feel because I couldn't see it. In an instant, there was sunlight shining into the darkened room. I opened the locked door and went outside in order to see the dials a little better. I had to see my location in time. Linda was gone and I had to get back to her.

In my haste to get outside, I had instinctively closed the door behind me. I heard the lock snap. I was locked out! The dials read: July 2, 1930, 12:30 p.m. I had accidentally moved two days ahead and it was early afternoon.

I decided to set the dials to June 30, a few moments after I had been knocked to the floor. Just as I was about to do this, a crowd of people came walking down the sidewalk. I didn't want to be near anyone for fear of transporting them with me, so I put the device in my pocket and started walking up the street looking for an isolated area.

As I was walking past a soup line, I heard a familiar voice call, "George!" It was Linda! Her long hair was all matted and she was filthy.

I asked, "What happened to you?"

She was almost in tears. "It was horrible! The police took all of us to a jailhouse where we spent the night in a crowded cell. The place was filthy and we had to sleep on the floor. When I was released the next morning, I went back to the hotel. I told the manager that you had the key and would he please let me in my room. He didn't believe me and asked me for identification. Since I didn't have any with me, he asked me to leave. I walked the streets after that and only got food because I found this soup line. I found a public toilet down in the subway so that I could relieve myself when I had to, and I slept in an alley last night."

I put my arms around her and pulled her close to comfort her. I said, "Let's go back to the hotel so that you can get cleaned up, and then we'll get something to eat. When we get back to the hotel I'm going to give the manager a piece of my mind."

"Please don't do that. I don't want to be embarrassed any more than I have been already. I just want to sneak in without him seeing me. He probably won't recognize me once I have gotten a bath and have changed into clean clothing."

Linda made me promise to do it her way, which I did. When we walked into the hotel lobby, the manager was not at his desk, so we quickly walked up the stairs to our room on the third floor without being seen. Linda went immediately into the bathroom and took a long bath.

When she came out, she said, "I feel really clean for the first time in two days."

After she put on clean clothes, we left the hotel and found a nice little restaurant. Linda ate as if she was starving to death. I asked if she would like to stay a few days more to make up for her horrible couple of days.

"We can't, George. You have to get back to work."

"Yes, we can. You're forgetting that I can control the time that we arrive home. We can stay away for a month and still return home on the Fourth of July."

She said, "Your invention is amazing. I think I would like to stay here a few days longer—as long as we stay away from dance halls and speakeasies. That should give us plenty of time to shop for antiques."

"Linda, we are going to watch a vintage Fourth of July celebration this weekend."

After a great weekend and a few extra days of shopping, we returned home with some small pieces of furniture. On Wednesday evening, we took them to the antique dealer and made a nice profit.

When we left the antique dealers, Linda asked, "George, why don't we travel farther back into the past? We could see how our ancestors lived and worked, and what they did for entertainment. It would be like living in history and it would be fun to go shopping for furniture. We could really have a great vacation."

"Where would you like to go?"

"Back to Colonial Philadelphia," she answered.

"We could go back. But the money for that time period would be very expensive. I don't think that we could make a profit on the furniture."

"What if we sold something to people back in that time period that caught their interest. We might even have something that they needed, and we could make enough money to buy furniture."

We thought about it for a while and decided on ballpoint pens. We knew that not all of the people back in Colonial times could read or write, but the pens would be a novelty. We could show them how to draw pictures with them and even supply them with some plain white writing paper, since that was also a scarce commodity.

I said, "We have to by some cheap pens that after they run out of ink they will be thrown away and not be around for future generations to find. The paper that we buy also has to be not of good quality. We don't want to change history."

Linda replied, "That is a very good idea. I would have never even given it a thought."

We decided to travel back to July 1765 and that a Saturday would be the best time to sell our pens. We thought that many people would be gathered near Market Street because it was a main shopping area. It was mid-summer and we hoped for good weather to sell our pens and paper. Most of all, it was before the Revolutionary War, and the economy had to be good.

On Tuesday after work, Linda and I went to a costume store and rented some Colonial clothing. Our next stop was at a local stationery store where we bought twelve dozen ballpoint pens with blue ink and four packs of white writing paper.

Finally our weekend adventure into 1765 was about to begin. After we transported, I carried the writing paper and Linda carried the pens to Market Street. We set up shop near some other merchants not far from the river. Just as we thought, there were a lot of people buying items from the merchants. A curious crowd gathered around us as I was writing and drawing on a sheet of paper. One gentleman asked, "How do those instruments work for writing? All that I have ever used were quills."

I replied, "These pens are a new invention and may someday take the place of quills. We are selling them for three pence each and you can also buy twenty sheets of paper for an extra three pence."

He became our first customer, purchasing a pen and twenty sheets of paper. I gave the coins to Linda to put in her apron pocket. I said, "Let's not shop for furniture with this money."

"Why aren't we buying furniture?" she asked. "I thought that was our plan."

"The coins that I just handed you are probably worth as much as—or more than—the antique value of the small pieces of furniture that we can take home. All we have to do is sell the coins to a coin dealer."

Linda said, "That sounds good—just keep handing me the coins and I'll tuck them away in my pocket for safekeeping."

By late morning, our ballpoint pens and paper were selling like hotcakes, and we had sold most of them when a British officer walked up to us. He asked, "Where did you get these writing instruments and paper?"

I answered, "We purchased them from a friend of mine. The pens are a new invention of his."

The officer said, "Let me see your bill of sale."

"I don't have it with me," I replied. "I left it at home."

He waved his hand and called some British soldiers who were standing nearby to come over. He said, "I am putting you under arrest until you can produce a receipt. I think that you are a thief and have stolen these items."

When he was going to arrest me, I quickly slipped Linda the time-transporting device without him seeing me because I thought that they might not search her. Then I said, "Sir, I am telling you the truth. I am not a thief!"

"You can prove that by producing a receipt," he replied.

I said, "My wife will have to go home and get it."

To my surprise, the officer said, "Your wife is not being charged with any offense. Send her home to fetch the receipt."

"Linda, would you please go home and get the receipt so that I can get out of this mess."

She knew that I meant to use the time-transporting device to get me out of jail. She said, "Yes, I will, but I must see where they are taking you so that I can give the receipt to the officer in charge."

The officer said, "That will be fine. You may follow us." He ordered his men to pick up the few papers and pens that were left as contraband, and take me to the jailhouse. Linda followed me to the jailhouse at Fourth and Market Streets. The officer allowed her to follow me to the jail cell and kiss me good-bye. That was the last that I saw of her until late that evening when she suddenly appeared in my jail cell holding the time-transporting device and a flashlight.

Linda said, "Quick, hold on to me!" She set the dials and we were moving through time. We stopped in a vacant lot in the middle of the night.

"Are we in the right place, Linda?"

"Yes. Follow me and hang on."

I held onto her arm and we walked off of the lot onto a red brick pavement next to a cobblestone street. She set the device again and we were transported to twenty-first century Market Street at around midnight.

"What took you so long to get me out of that place?" I asked.

"I stood outside of the building until there were no people around, so that I could set the device without anyone seeing me. When the area was clear, I moved the dials to midnight and moved slowly forward in time."

"That was a good idea to bring a flashlight."

"I remembered your predicament at the dance hall and I'm glad that we parked the car close by. I took the flashlight out of the glove compartment where you keep it. The flashlight came in handy to read the dials on the device at night."

"Did you have any problems with the device?"

"I have watched you several times and it seemed fairly easy. I moved backward in time until there was a vacant lot where the jailhouse had once stood. Then I walked onto the lot and moved the dials on the device slowly backward again. As I was moving the dials, the jailhouse started to appear. Then I walked slowly into your cell until you appeared, and then I stopped."

Linda handed me the device and we walked back to our car. As I drove home, she asked, "What happened to you at the jailhouse?"

"The officer that arrested me questioned me for about two hours. He seemed more concerned about the blue ink in the pens, and the type and quality of the paper. He wanted to know where everything was made. He asked me what type of material was used to make the pens. I told him that it was called plastic. Unable to understand what plastic was, he asked me if the pens were some type of a weapon that could be used by the colonists. I told him that a pen was a weapon, because it was mightier than a sword. He didn't seem to like my answer and with a nasty tone told one of his soldiers, 'Put him back in the cell until he is ready to talk. I think that this man is up to some mischief and is withholding important information.'

What happened to the money that we made on the sale of the pens and paper?"

"I have it. They never asked me for it. We can still sell it to a coin dealer."

After we arrived home, I walked immediately in the direction of my workshop with the device.

Linda asked, "Where are you going with the device, George?"

"I'm going to go into my shop and disassemble this thing."

"Tomorrow we are going to the bank to put the gyroscope in our safe deposit box, and then we are going to a coin dealer to sell the money. We are getting into too much trouble with that gyroscope. We could wind up getting lost somewhere in time and not be able to get back home."

"I think that you may be right," she replied. "I was worried that I wouldn't be able to get you out of that jail. I could have lost you forever. If space travelers left that gyroscope here, maybe they didn't intend it to be used in a time-transporting device. It may have another purpose. I know that with your curiosity, someday you will figure it out and want to use it in another one of your inventions.

***

THE BARN DOOR

My name is Tomas Carson. I write and illustrate short stories for children and I am fairly successful. I'm thirty years old and single. My parents tell me that I should devote some time to look for a wife, and I always tell them that right now I am too busy with my career to bother.

Recently I decided that working in Philadelphia was too noisy and crowed for me to concentrate. I needed to have someplace quiet and peaceful in the suburban countryside, so I made arrangements with a realtor by the name of Janet Stanley. Her office is located in Whitpain Township, and she had a listing of properties for sale that she thought might interest me.

I met Janet at her office on a nice sunny Monday morning at the beginning of April. Janet told me that she wanted to escort me through a house in Whitpain Township that she thought would be just right for me. She showed me to her car and we drove to a farmhouse about two miles from Route 73.

The farmhouse was very old and even had a barn located about fifty feet away. Janet told me that the house and barn had been built in 1768. The house looked as if it had been very well kept. The outside walls were painted light brown with dark brown shutters on the windows. There was a new oil heating system in the basement and a large fireplace in the family room. The original hand-cut ceiling beams protruded and they were visible between the finished sheetrock ceilings in all of the rooms. All of the sheetrock ceilings were painted white to enhance the dark brown beams. The kitchen and bathrooms were modern and up to date. This was exactly the house that I wanted. In fact, I thought that it was perfect!

Next we inspected the barn. It was in great shape for its age and it was also painted light brown. The interior ceiling beams were made of evenly sized tree trunks.

I said, "Those ceiling beams are different. I've never seen a ceiling like that."

Janet replied, "Most of the old barns in this area that I have seen were made this way. I think that it was because the tree trunks were the strongest piece of lumber that they could use at the time of construction, due to their limited resources. They probably would have supported the weight of the bales of hay and feed stored on the second floor. I have seen stalls in many of these old barns on the first floor so I assume that is where they kept the horses."

When we walked out of the barn, Janet said, "The entire lot covers three acres and most of the trees that surround it block the view of the farm next door. It was once part of the property and was sold off years ago to a private farmer when the seller's grandfather retired."

I decided to make an offer on the property, which Janet passed on to the seller. A few days later, she called and told me that my offer was accepted. I was elated! It seemed like the perfect place to escape from all the noise and crowded environment of the city.

I moved into my new old house in middle of May. Once I had settled in, I decided to check out the barn and see if there was anything that I could do to improve it. After looking it over, I thought that the only thing that I could do was use it for storage. I could park the car inside when it snows in the winter. I'd also need a snow blower and a lawnmower.

The main large barn door entrance was on the same side as the front door of the house, which did not face the road. There was another large barn door on the opposite side that faced the paved single-lane road. The door was locked with a large rusty old-fashioned padlock that looked to be at least a hundred years old. It was connected to the door by a heavy steel hasp that was also rusted.

There was a large white sign on the door with black skull and crossbones. Under the skull and crossbones was painted in bold black letters, "Never Open This Door."

I didn't care much about the ridiculous sign on the door and had no idea why anyone would put it on there. I was only interested in getting the door open so that I could drive in from the road when there was inclement weather and park my car in the barn.

I looked around the barn for a key, but I couldn't find one. I went into the house and still found no key. I decided to look in the basement for a key or a tool to open the lock and found an old sledgehammer in the corner. I went back into the barn and hit the lock with a couple of good bangs; it broke and fell on the floor. I pried open the hasp and tried to move the door, but it would not budge. I walked around the barn to the other side of the door to see if there was another lock. There was and I removed it in the same way. I put the sledgehammer down and tried to open the door, but could not because there was no door handle, and the door opened from the inside. I left the sledgehammer on the ground and walked around through the barn to the other side of the door and gave it a good pull. The rollers on the track above moved the door quite easily and, to my surprise, the door opened without any problem.

I looked down, but my sledgehammer was missing. *Who would come by and steal an old sledgehammer that fast?*

I looked up and the single-lane road was gone too—replaced by a dirt road! *Where are the electric company's poles and wires?* I ran around the outside of the barn to the front door and looked in. A horse was standing inside a stall! There was a bale of hay on the floor and the back door was closed. The house and barn looked different. They were painted white. My car was missing and there were only some wagon tracks in the ground where the driveway should have been. When I saw a farmer with a horse-drawn plow working in the field beyond the tree line, I thought that I had to be hallucinating.

I was so shaken that I ran to the back door of the barn. It was open! I looked inside and it was the same as I had left it, with no horse, and no bale of hay. I ran in and slammed the door shut. I found a spike on the floor and closed the hasp on the door, jamming the spike through the loop in the hasp, ensuring that no one could get in.

Still shaking, I walked out of the barn and looked around. There was no farmer with a horse drawn plow in the field. The house and barn were painted light brown, and my car was parked in the driveway. I walked slowly around to the back door of the barn, and found it closed. The road was paved with asphalt and the electric company's poles, and wires were in place. When I looked down, I found my sledgehammer lying where I had left it. I picked it up and walked slowly back to the house, trying to figure out what had just happened to me.

Inside the house, I sat in my favorite reclining chair, trying to calm down. *What has just happened to me? I'm not going nuts. What then? The answer seems obvious, but it doesn't make any sense. Somehow I have traveled back in time. Maybe the old man that lived here did too. That would explain the warning sign on the barn door.* After a few deep breaths, I decided to take a calmer approach to the situation. All that I had seen was a farmer in the field and a horse in the barn—and neither of them looked threatening. The farmer didn't even notice me. I could go back. No, I should go back. This could be the find of the century. I couldn't pass it up because of some childish fear of the unknown.

The next morning after breakfast, I went out into the barn, pulled the spike out of the hasp, and opened that mysterious barn door. The first thing that greeted me was the dirt road, wagon wheel tracks, and shoe marks made by horses in the soft ground. I noticed that the electric poles were missing.

I heard birds singing in the trees across the road. They looked the same as the birds on the other side of the barn. If Mother Nature hadn't changed anything, I guessed that my best bet for finding out what year I was in was to stand by the door and wait. If I was in any danger, I could always slam it shut.

After half an hour, I heard what sounded like a team of horses racing down the road, getting closer to the barn. I pulled the door until it was only open five or six inches so that I could see what was going on outside. The noise was a team of horses and they were pulling a stagecoach. It stopped right in front of the barn.

The driver was wearing a three-corner black hat, a Colonial black jacket, and breeches. He got down from his seat and opened the stagecoach door. I heard him say, "You better get out, miss, and hide in the woods. It is your best chance to get away. They are going to catch up with us soon and take you prisoner."

A young woman wearing a Colonial hoop skirt and a matching blue bonnet climbed out. She seemed to be well dressed and didn't look like the type of person that would be running from the law. She appeared to be under quite a bit of stress and in a hurry to get away when she said, "Thank you for your help." She ran into the woods across the road.

The driver climbed back up on the stagecoach and proceeded to race up the road. Five minutes later, I heard more horses coming down the road toward the barn. As they passed the barn, I could see about ten or twelve British soldiers in red uniforms racing at full gallop. After they had gone by, I noticed the young woman hiding behind a tree across the road. I opened the barn door and motioned to her by waving my hand to come over. She just looked at me and didn't move.

I started running in her direction and shouted, "Hurry, please come with me. I'll hide you."

When I got close, I said, "I won't harm you or turn you in to the soldiers. We must hurry before they return." She came out from behind the tree and I followed her to the barn, making sure that she didn't stumble as she ran. When she was safely inside, I slammed the door shut and put the spike back in the hasp.

I said, "You will be safe in here."

She looked at me as if I were crazy and asked, "How will I be safe in here when the other door is wide open?"

"Trust me," I replied. Before I uttered another word, I took a good look at her. She was beautiful with long brown hair tucked up under her bonnet, brown eyes, and the face of an angel.

"Why are you staring at me, sir?"

"Because you are beautiful."

"Thank you for the compliment, but it will not help you when the British turn around and search this barn. They will probably hang you from the nearest tree—and God only knows what they will do to me. Why are you wearing such strange clothing?"

"I'm just wearing a sweat shirt, jeans, and sneakers," I answered.

"I guess they do look a little strange to you. Let me introduce myself. My name's Thomas Carson. What's yours?"

"Barbara Hill," she answered.

Before we could say another word, we heard the sound of horses racing back down the road toward the barn.

"Oh my God," she whispered. "We are caught with no place to hide! I should have stayed in the woods. I could have hidden behind the trees."

"Trust me," I said. "We are safe here in my barn. The soldiers won't be able to see us."

"I must be in this barn talking to a madman. We are not invisible, sir!"

"Yes, we are," I replied. I sat on an old bench that was near the interior barn wall.

Barbara stood for a moment and then sat down on the bench next to me, probably thinking that I was totally out of my mind as we waited in silence.

We heard the British soldiers dismount outside of the barn door. Then one of them said, "Colonel Monroe, sir, this door will not open."

Colonel Monroe replied, "See if there is a door on the other side of the barn. The coach driver said that she got off near this farm. Search the barn! Some of you search the woods across the road. Fetch that farmer out in the field so that I can question him, and make sure that you do a thorough search of his house."

Barbara trembled next to me as she waited. About five minutes went by and, still trembling, she asked, "Where are they? What is taking them so long to come in?"

I replied, "We are talking loud enough. I don't think they can hear us."

She looked at me and seemed puzzled at my ridiculous remark, probably wishing that she had remained hiding in the woods.

After about twenty minutes, we heard the British soldiers mounting their horses near the rear barn door. One soldier said, "There is no one in the barn except for a horse and lots of hay, and feed for the animals. We have also searched in the woods, sir, and there is no sign of her."

Another man said, "She is not hiding in the house. We have searched everywhere, sir."

Colonel Monroe replied, "I would think that she made it off into the woods on foot. She has to eat and sleep somewhere. That woman will not make a fool out of me! After we catch her and get my documents, we will hang her on the spot. I would love to see her dangling at the end of a rope. Let us move on and check some of the other nearby farmhouses."

I said, "That man really hates you. What documents does he want from you and why is he so angry?"

Barbara looked at me without giving an answer and then turned away, burying her head in her hands, probably wondering what was happening.

After the soldiers left, Barbara asked, "Are they insane? There is no horse or hay in this barn. They had to walk right past us. Can't they see? Why couldn't we see them?"

I answered, "They did walk past us, but it was over two hundred years ago."

She just looked confused.

I asked, "What is today's date?"

"It is May 20, 1778," she replied.

I said, "Try to have an open mind about what I am going to tell you. That barn door is an opening to a time portal."

She looked puzzled. I explained what had happened to me when I opened the door and how shaken up I was after I went through the doorway.

I said, "Barbara, welcome to May 20, 2009."

Barbara looked at me with a very serious look on her beautiful face and asked, "Do you practice witchcraft, Thomas?"

The question struck me as funny and I started to laugh.

"Why are you laughing? I have heard that witches can cast spells on crowds of people and become invisible, and no one can see them. Is that what you did to the soldiers, Thomas?"

"No, I am not a witch and I'm sorry. I shouldn't have laughed. You must think it strange of me to tell you that you have just walked over two hundred years into the future." I took her by the hand and said, "Come with me." We walked out of the barn and stood near the back door.

"What has happened to the road?" she asked. "It is covered with some kind of paving, and where did those tree trunks come from that are connected to each other by ropes? I have to get out of here! I have important documents to deliver. Please let me go, Thomas."

I said, "I can let you out the back door and you can return to May 20, 1778, and the soldiers will capture you, and you will never deliver your documents. Please consider staying here for at least a few days or until it is safe for you to return. This is what the future looks like to me and it is quite normal. The road has been here for over two hundred years, but now it's paved with blacktop. Those wooden poles support electric power lines. We use the power from the lines to light our homes. It is called electricity and it powers many of our appliances. An inventor that you may have heard of was the first to experiment with it. His name was Benjamin Franklin."

"Yes, I know him, and I have met him. He is very active in our revolution. Is he here?"

"No. He died over two hundred years ago. He was a great statesman and our ambassador to France. He lived in Philadelphia and is buried there, but don't worry, once you go through the barn door and return to 1778, he will be alive and well. Come with me and let me show you more."

As we walked toward the house, she asked, "What is that shiny big black metal thing with the funny wheels?"

"That's my car. They were invented over a hundred years ago. We have developed them a great deal since then. They have replaced the horse as a means of travel. I'll take you for a ride in it if you have to stay here for a while."

At that moment, she shrieked, "What is that thing in the sky making all of that noise? It is some kind of monster coming to kill us!"

"Don't be afraid. It's only an airplane carrying passengers to their destination."

"Where are the people?"

"They are inside of the airplane in comfortable seats."

"Where are they going?"

"I don't know. Maybe they are traveling from Philadelphia to California."

"Where is California—and how can that airplane fly?"

"I'll explain all of that later. I think that you should stay here until it is safe enough for you to leave. I have a guest bedroom that you can sleep in while you are here."

"Thank you for the invitation, Thomas. It will be much better than sleeping in the woods until the British patrols have stopped looking for me."

As we were walking into the house, I told Barbara not to be afraid of all of the things that she was about to see. First, I showed Barbara all of the appliances. She thought that the television was a magic box and kept looking behind it for the people on the screen. The electric range was something from hell.

I remarked, "I guess that means that you won't be cooking."

I showed her upstairs to the guest room and told her that would be her room while she stayed with me. Then I showed her how all of the appliances in the bathroom worked, which totally amazed her. She kept flushing the toilet like a child with a new toy.

I said, "I'll get you some fresh towels and you can take a bath or a shower, whichever you prefer, now that you know how to work everything. I've got some extra pajamas and a robe that you can wear."

"I am fine the way I am," she said. "I took a bath the other day."

"We take a bath or a shower at least once a day. Cleanliness is next to Godliness."

"But we will waste the water."

"Don't worry. We have plenty of it."

"I have one question that I would like to ask you. Why were those soldiers chasing you and what kind of documents do you have that are so important to them?"

"I am a spy for General George Washington, and I am proud of it. You may have never heard of him, but he is a great general and a wonderful man.

I pulled a dollar bill from my wallet and showed her the portrait of George Washington. "Is this the man that you are working for?"

She looked at the bill and answered with a question, "Where did you get this?"

"He is on our currency because he was the first president of our United States of America." I removed a ten-dollar bill from my wallet and gave it to Barbara. "Here is another man that you may know. His name is Alexander Hamilton. After George Washington became president he appointed him Secretary of the United States Treasury. Now get washed and dressed and come downstairs when you are ready, and I'll tell you more."

Barbara gave me a dumbfounded obedient look and said, "All right."

I was sitting in my reclining chair watching television when Barbara came down the stairs in my pajamas, robe, and slippers. With her long brown hair falling down to the middle of her back, she looked like a goddess. I couldn't keep my eyes off of her.

"What are you looking at, Thomas?"

"I'm looking at a beautiful woman standing in front of me wearing my pajamas," I answered.

"Well do not get any ideas, sir, or I will be sleeping in the barn tonight," she said. "Why are those women running around almost naked on that magic box?"

"I'm watching the news and they are on the beach in their new swimwear. The clothes that women wear are quite different than the clothing that you are used to seeing."

"I do not know if I could get accustomed to that," she said.

"I hope that you won't have to stay with me that long. We will have to keep checking the road behind the barn daily for British patrols. Hopefully it will be safe enough for you to leave soon."

I made some sandwiches for lunch. After we ate, I turned on the History Channel for Barbara and showed her how to use the remote. I thought that she could get some idea of what had happened over the last two hundred years. While she was watching television, I went into my office and started to work on my new book. I thought that it would be a good idea to write about time travel, since the subject might interest my young readers.

Hours later, when I came out of my office, Barbara was still watching television. It looked as if she had become a pro with the remote, because she was channel surfing.

"Thomas, did you know that we beat the British and won our independence, and now they are the best of friends with us?"

"Yes. A lot has happened over the last two hundred years. I'm getting hungry. Would you like something to eat?"

"Yes," she answered.

"I have some frozen dinners. Would you like chicken or beef?'

"I would like chicken," she answered. "But I cannot eat it frozen!"

"I'm going to nuke it in the microwave. Do you want me to show you how it works?"

"Yes," she answered. Barbara was a very intent student trying to learn everything about the microwave oven.

When it started to get dark, Barbara asked, "Where are your candles, Thomas? I will light them for you."

"We don't use candles for light. The only use we have for them is for decoration, or we buy special scented candles for their smells. We have electric lights. Let me show you how to turn them on."

I showed her how to flip the switches on and off in each room. If anyone were passing by the house, they must have thought that I was sending out S. O. S. signals because Barbara was experimenting with all of the light switches in the house. She kept flipping them on and off for about fifteen minutes.

The next morning after breakfast, I said, "I laid out a pair of jeans, a sweatshirt, and some undergarments on the bed in your room. They belong to my sister. She left them at my townhouse in the city when she was staying with me. My sister is about your size and I think that they will fit you. I have to pick up some groceries at the store. If you would like to go with me, all that you have to do is change into her clothing."

Barbara went up into her room to try on the clothing. Then she shouted, "These things that you call jeans look like trousers that a man wears. Do women really wear these things?"

"Yes. Don't let it worry you. You will look like a lot of other women and will blend in with the crowd. If you were to wear the clothing that you arrived in, everyone would look at you. They would probably think that you were going to a costume party."

Barbara looked great when she came downstairs and walked into the family room wearing my sister's clothing. She looked as if she belonged in 2009.

I couldn't help saying, "You are a very beautiful woman."

"Thank you for the compliment," she replied.

We decided to check what was happening behind the barn door before we went shopping for groceries. After we walked into the barn, I slowly cracked the rear barn door open. We could see a British patrol coming up the road, so I closed the door quickly and dropped the spike back in the hasp.

Barbara said, "I would guess that they have not given up their search for me."

"It doesn't look that way. We may as well go shopping."

Barbara and I walked to my car. I helped her in and clipped her seatbelt.

"What is this for?"

"To hold you in place in case we were to get into an accident."

"How could we get into an accident?"

"You'll see. Just wait until you see all of the traffic on the roads. Cover your eyes if you are afraid."

I started the engine and, as the car was moving forward, Barbara began to get a little nervous and held on to the dash. After a minute or two, she let go. When she saw the other vehicles on Route 73, Barbara put her hands over her eyes. She started to spread her fingers in curiosity and peep at the other cars and trucks.

"What are those big long square conveyances with all of the wheels, and those other long conveyances with the big windows and wheels?"

"The big square vehicles are called trucks and they carry all types of things from food to furniture. The vehicles with all of the windows are buses and they carry people as passengers. We also have trains that run on steel rails that carry almost anything,"

As I drove to a shopping center a few miles east on Route 73, Barbara was impressed by all of the houses. I told her that this was only the suburban area of Philadelphia, and that there were many more houses and commercial buildings in the city.

The shopping center was another experience. It started with the supermarket and the shopping cart, and then it escalated. Barbara couldn't get over the way that most of the food was packaged. She didn't understand how the food was put in sealed cans. The plastic bottles were even more of a challenge. She accidentally knocked a bottle of grape juice on the floor and wanted to know why the glass didn't break. After I gave her a long explanation on just about everything that she picked up in the store, I think that she sort of understood. It seemed as if I was teaching her Food Shopping 101.

When we carried everything back to the car and packed it into the trunk, Barbara said, "It is just like the trunk on the stagecoach. All of my clothing was in it. I hope that the driver stored them for me until I return."

"I would guess that he will be in deep trouble if he sold them."

"He certainly will. I paid a lot of hard-earned money for my clothing."

Just as I was ready to help Barbara into my car, she spied a women's clothing store. "Thomas, can we look at the clothing in that store?"

"Yes, I guess that we should. You will probably need a few changes of clothing if you have to stay with me for a while. It looks like the British aren't going to give up searching for you. Let me do the talking when we go into the store. I'll have to make up a story to tell the salesperson. I don't want to spill the beans."

"All right, but why would you want to spill beans?"

"It's just a form of slang that we use. It just means that I'm not going to let anyone know where you are from, or they might want to put me on the funny farm."

"What is a funny farm?"

Almost breaking into laughter, I answered, "I'll tell you later."

After we walked into the store, I went over to a saleswoman about Barbara's age. I told her that all of my friend's clothing had been burned in a fire, and that she needed everything. The saleswoman said, "That is a tragic shame, honey. Come with me and I'll get you set up with everything that you need." Barbara followed her obediently while looking around in amazement at everything in the large store.

Barbara came out of the dressing room modeling dresses, slacks, blouses, shoes, jackets, and pocketbooks. She looked beautiful in everything. Finally, after almost two hours they were done picking out everything that she needed to look like a twenty-first-century woman.

The saleswoman put everything in shopping bags to make it easier for us to carry. Then I gave her my charge card for a very large bill. As we were leaving, Barbara asked me why I gave everyone a card instead of currency. I told her that a credit card was just like currency—only it was buy now, pay later.

"I guess it is like having credit with the local merchant."

"Exactly the same."

After we returned to the house and had put the groceries in the pantry and the clothing in Barbara's room, she said, "Thank you, Thomas, for everything that you have done for me, and the clothing that you have bought for me. I truly appreciate your kindness."

I couldn't resist the urge, so I pulled her close and kissed her. To my surprise, Barbara pulled me even closer and returned my kiss. When we moved apart she said, "We should not be doing this. It is not proper. We are not engaged."

I pulled her close again, held her in my arms, and whispered, "Does it really matter?" I like you very much."

"I also like you very much, Thomas," she replied, and then we kissed again.

Each morning, we checked for British patrols and found that they were still searching for her. It seemed as if they were never going to give up their search. I knew the documents that Barbara was carrying must have been very important to them.

While Barbara was staying with me, she told me that she knew how to cook, so I taught her how to use the appliances. Barbara had a very good education and could read the cookbooks. She made some delicious meals and told me that it was her way of paying me back for my kindness and allowing her stay in my home.

One morning after we had been checking the road for almost two weeks, we found no British patrols in sight. Barbara said, "Thomas, it looks as if it is safe enough for me to leave now. I must deliver the documents that I have in my possession to General Washington."

"I know," I replied. If she were to stay any longer, I knew that we would fall in love and that seemed at the time the wrong thing to do.

Barbara went back into the house and changed into her blue dress and bonnet. As we were kissing good-bye at the barn door, we heard the sounds of men and horses. It sounded as if an entire army was out on the road behind the barn door.

We heard a voice on the other side of the barn door shout, "Captain Barrington, give the order for the men to camp here on this farm! We have plenty of food and water in this area. As soon as the camp is set up, I want all of your men to start searching the woods, houses, and barns immediately. We will find that woman. I want to see the fear on her face when I hang her."

Another voice shouted, "Yes, sir, Colonel Mason!"

Barbara whispered, "Thomas, I think that I may have to stay with you a little while longer. It is going to be impossible for me to leave with British troops camped here."

"Stay as long as you want—at least until it is safe enough for you to leave." Inside, I was thinking that maybe I really didn't want her to leave at all.

We walked back to the house holding hands. Barbara went up to her room where she changed into her jeans, a short sleeve top, and sneakers.

When she came into the family room where I was watching the morning news, I looked up at her and said, "You look really beautiful."

Blushing, she replied, "Thank you for the compliment, Thomas. You certainly know how to say nice things to a woman—and I really do appreciate them."

I walked over to her and put my arms around her small waist. I pulled her close and she put her arms around my shoulders. Soon we were locked in a passionate embrace, returning each other's kisses as if we were newlyweds.

When we separated for a moment, I whispered, "This may sound selfish, but I really didn't want you to leave."

"I felt the same way," whispered Barbara. "But you have to understand that I must complete my mission when Colonel Mason and his troops are gone."

"I know. But for the time that we have together, let us enjoy each other's company. The British soldiers don't exist in my time period. So what would you say if I asked you to take a walk with me across the road in back of my barn and explore that wooded area where I first saw you?"

"I would say yes. I would very much like to go exploring with you, Thomas." As we walked past the barn, she said, "I cannot hear the soldiers on the other side of the barn."

"I know. I think that we have to be inside the barn to hear them."

Barbara squeezed my hand tightly and said, "We will not be going back in there today." She squeezed my hand even tighter as we headed toward the road. When she saw that the road was paved with asphalt and no one was on it, she released her tight grip on my hand, realizing that we were safe.

About a hundred yards into the woods, we came to a large clearing with a small stream running through it. We sat down on the bank and talked about our lives. She wanted to know about my life, my family, and what I did for a living. I told her all that I could remember about my family life, my parents, my sister, and about my work as a writer of children's books. Barbara seemed impressed with the fact that I wrote stories for children, and said that she thought it was wonderful that a man would do something like that.

She told me about her life. She had been only seven years old when her mother died. After her mother passed away, her father raised her. He made sure that she went to school and received a good education. When she was eighteen, her father was in the wrong place at the wrong time. Some citizens were taunting British soldiers near an armory. Barbara's father was walking by when the soldiers opened fire on the crowd, killing him instantly. After his death, she was on her own. When the revolution started, she became a spy for the Colonial Army.

Tears started to fill Barbara's eyes as she finished telling me about her life. I pulled her close and tried to console her, knowing that it was hard for her to talk about her past.

After a few moments of silence, Barbara kissed me on the cheek. Then she pulled away, grabbed my hand, and got up. She pulled on my hand and ordered, "Come on. Get up, Thomas! We are going back to the house and I am going to make you a delicious beef stew for dinner. It was one of my mother's recipes and I know that you will like it. You have all of the ingredients in your kitchen and I love cooking for you."

As we passed the barn, she pulled me inside. "I want to listen at the door for a moment. Maybe I can find out how long the troops will be staying."

After about five minutes, we heard a horse suddenly gallop up near the door. The rider said to a nearby sentry, "Where is Colonel Mason? I have important orders for him."

"He is in the tent on the other side of the road, sir. I will inform him that you are here."

A few moments later, we heard Colonel Mason's voice. "Why are you here and what do you want, Lieutenant?"

"Here, sir, these documents are for you. They are written orders from the general. He has ordered Captain Barrington and I to return immediately with all of the men that you have in your command except for fifty foot soldiers. The general said that it is ridiculous for you to continue searching for this woman with an entire battalion. He has a war to fight and needs these men on the front lines."

Colonel Mason replied, "I have to find the woman. She is a spy and I need these troops to flush her out."

The lieutenant said, "The general's orders are very clear, sir. If you disobey them, you will be court-martialed."

Colonel Mason shouted, "Sentry, find Captain Barrington and tell him to pull all of the troops out except for fifty of the best foot soldiers and leave with the lieutenant immediately."

"Yes, sir, Colonel," the sentry replied.

"They are finally leaving," said Barbara.

I replied, "Colonel Mason still has fifty men and you have to wait until they have left the area before you can deliver your documents to General Washington."

"I know that I will have to wait a little longer. I will be checking every day until Colonel Mason leaves the area. Meanwhile let us go into the house and I will make you the beef stew that I promised."

At dinner, I said, "Barbara, this is the best beef stew that I have ever tasted in my life."

"I knew that you would like it. My father liked it so much that he could have eaten it every day."

Each morning we would go into the barn and check to see if the soldiers had left, and then we would walk through the woods to the clearing and sit by the stream. We would talk about our life experiences and anything that amused us. We had only one problem—we were happy being with each other and had fallen in love.

Three days later, Colonel Mason and his soldiers finally left their encampment on the farm. We opened the door slightly so that we could see which way they were going. Barbara said, "They are marching in the direction that they originally came from and the road will soon be clear for me to deliver the documents to General Washington."

That evening, Barbara came into my room and got into bed with me. We slept together locked in each other's arms.

The next morning after breakfast, Barbara looked at me and said tearfully, "Thomas, I must leave."

Her words hit me like a bolt of lightning! "Why? We won the war."

"Because I must deliver the documents that I have to General Washington. They are so important that if I do not deliver them, I may change history."

"You are here living in the future and everything is all right."

"I know that it is at this moment. I have been thinking what would happen if I do not go back to my time and something changes because I did not deliver the documents? What if you were never born because I did not finish my mission? Can you understand that I must go back, Thomas?"

Tears rolled down my cheeks. "Yes," I said. It was only a partial lie. Intellectually, I knew that she had to go back, but my heart didn't agree.

Barbara pulled me close, buried her head on my chest, and started to cry. When she regained some of her composure, she sobbed, "I love you, Thomas, and I do not want to leave you, but I must."

"Please let me come with you."

"No! It may still change history as you know it."

Unable to speak, I pulled her close as tears streamed down my cheeks. Finally we separated and Barbara went up to her room, and changed into the clothing that she was wearing when we first met. We walked to the barn door without saying a word. I opened the barn door and we kissed in a tight embrace. After we said good-bye, we separated and she walked up the road. I felt as if my world was coming to an end and watched until she was out of sight.

I was ready to close the barn door when I looked down the road in the other direction. In the distance, I could see Colonel Mason returning with his soldiers at a fast pace. I knew what he was up too! He had probably suspected that she was hiding somewhere near the barn and had posted a spy to tell him when she had left her hiding place.

I had to save her, but what could I do against fifty armed soldiers? I had no weapons. I closed the barn door and ran out of the barn to find something that I could use for a weapon and then I saw it in my driveway. My car! I got in and started the engine and drove it into the barn. I got out and cracked the barn door open so that I could see when the troops had passed the barn. After they had all passed and marched three hundred yards up the road, it was time for me to use my weapon.

I opened the barn door, got into the car, and raced out of the barn and up the dirt road. When I was about fifty yards away from the troops, I started blowing the horn. When they turned and saw a metal monster coming after them, the men started dropping their muskets and running in all different directions to get out of the way. Colonel Mason's horse bolted and jumped, throwing him to the ground. I was hoping that he had broken his neck, but when I looked in the rearview mirror, I could see him struggling to get to his feet and catch his horse.

I drove as fast as I could over the bumpy road until I saw Barbara walking on the road. I blew the horn and, when she turned and saw me, she stopped. I pulled up alongside of her and shouted, "Get in."

Barbara was angry and shouted as she was getting into the car, "Why are you here, Thomas, and why are you driving in this car?"

"I am here to save your life! Colonel Mason and his soldiers waited until you left your hiding place in order to catch you. My car was the only weapon that I had that could scare the daylights out of him and his men. I'm going to drop you off at General Washington's camp. How far is it from here?"

Barbara started to calm down. "About a day's walk up this road."

"I should be able to make it in about an hour. Colonel Mason and his soldiers won't be able to catch us and maybe we can have General Washington set a trap for him."

"There is only one problem, Thomas. We cannot drive this car into the general's camp."

"We will have to hide it somewhere a short distance away and walk to the camp."

Most of the area that we were driving through was covered with thick forest, but occasionally we passed a farm or a farmhouse off in the distance. I was relieved that there was no wagon or horse traffic and no one walking on the road. I didn't want to scare anyone with my car. After an hour, Barbara said, "We are near the camp."

I found a spot in the woods just off of the road where I could hide the car. We covered it with loose brush so that it could not be seen by anyone passing by on the road.

As we were walking up the road, she said, "The camp is just around that bend ahead of us. Your clothing is a little strange so if anyone asks why you are dressed that way, I hope that you will be able to be creative."

"Don't worry. I'll think of something," I replied.

When we reached the campsite, we walked up to one of the sentries.

"My name is Barbara Hill, and the man with me is my escort, Thomas Carson. I must speak to General Washington."

The sentry looked at me and didn't say anything. Then he replied, "The general has been expecting you, Miss Hill; please follow me to his tent."

I was feeling a little nervous because I had never expected to meet

George Washington in person. This was about to become one of the greatest moments of my life. The sentry stopped in front of the tent and said, "General Washington, sir, Miss Hill and her escort have arrived." I could feel my heart beating with rapid anticipation.

General Washington emerged from the tent wearing slippers, a white shirt, and military breeches. He was tall and looked almost exactly like some of the portraits that I have seen—only younger and he wasn't wearing a wig.

He said, "Please excuse my appearance, Miss Hill. I wasn't expecting you." He looked at me oddly and asked, "Who is your friend?"

"This is Thomas Carson, a local farmer that helped hide me from Colonel Mason and his soldiers."

I was trembling with excitement and could hardly get any words out. Finally, I said, "I have heard so much about you and I am very happy to finally meet you, sir, and please excuse me for my appearance. When Colonel Mason and his men searched my farm looking for Miss Hill, they tore up my clothing just for their own amusement. I had to make what I am wearing out of the remnants of some material that I had stored away."

General Washington replied, "It looks like you did a fairly good job. I did not know that men could do such fine stitching. Do you make flags, Thomas?"

I hope he doesn't want me to take Betsy Ross's job away from her.

"No sir. I don't. Making the clothes that I am wearing was hard enough."

Barbara said, "Gentlemen, I need a little privacy. May I use your tent, sir? The documents that I have for you are hidden in my clothing."

"Yes, you may."

General Washington closed the flap behind her as she walked in. Barbara came out in a few moments and handed him the documents. When he looked at them, he said, "I cannot thank you enough, Miss Hill. You have done a splendid job and may have saved thousands of lives. I only wish that I could capture Colonel Mason. I have heard that he trusted you and the documents that you gave me came out of his desk. That man is ruthless and he will search until he finds you."

I said, "Sir, you can capture Colonel Mason. He is marching quickly up the road in pursuit of Miss Hill with a force of only fifty foot soldiers. I don't think that he knows that you have part of your army camped here. At the pace that they are moving, I would estimate that they are two hours' march from here."

His eyes lit up and he called out to one of his sentries, "Summon Captain Lewis! Tell him that I need him immediately."

A few moments later, Captain Lewis joined us and asked, "General Washington, what can I do for you, sir?"

The general replied, "I want you to take two hundred of our best men and, if at all possible, take Colonel Monroe alive. He is about two hours down the road with fifty soldiers. He has been pursuing Miss Hill, and now it is his turn to be the hunted."

Captain Lewis said, "I think that I can handle the task without too much difficulty, sir. I will leave at once."

Within five minutes, Captain Lewis had his men assembled and marching down the road.

General Washington said, "It would be best if you both stayed here until it is safe for you to go back on the road. I can have some men escort you after this skirmish is over."

I replied, "Thank you for the escort, sir, but I don't think that we will need one. My farm is only a short distance down the road. However, we will stay here until Captain Lewis comes back from his mission."

General Washington said, "I don't get much company except for my men so why don't we sit in the shade on that bench under the old oak tree yonder and chat for a while until Captain Lewis returns. I have some fine French wine that General Lafayette gave me when he visited last month."

Barbara said, "I think that would be very pleasant. Don't you agree, Thomas?"

I was thinking that I would love to stay chatting with George Washington for a month. "Yes, I can't think of anything that I would rather do than chat with General Washington."

We sat under the oak tree drinking wine while General Washington talked about his life. I had read about his life in history books, but this was different. He was describing everything in his own words.

I was totally fascinated. The hours flew by before Captain Lewis interrupted our conversation.

I didn't even notice that he had walked up and was standing in front of us until he said, "General Washington, we have taken Colonel Monroe and all of his men prisoner without firing a shot."

"Good work, Captain. How did you accomplish that feat?"

"I had several of our men go in advance of my troops to spy. When they spotted Colonel Monroe and his men, they reported back to me. My soldiers and I took cover in the woods on both sides of the road and waited until he and his men were between our lines. We came out with our muskets pointed at them and I told them to surrender or we would fire. Seeing that he was outnumbered, he shouted to his men to lay down their weapons and surrendered his sword to me."

Barbara asked, "Can I speak to Colonel Monroe, Captain Lewis?"

"Yes," he replied. With a large grin on his face, he said, "This should be interesting. I would like to know what you are going to say to him. He has been babbling about some secret weapon that we are using that chased him and his men off of the road. I personally think that the man has gone mad."

We followed Captain Lewis to a large open area at the center of the camp where Colonel Monroe and his men were sitting on the ground. Barbara walked over to the colonel, looked down at him, and said, "You wanted to have me hanged and watch me struggle to catch my last breath, didn't you? Now look at you like a fish in a bowl with no place for you to run and hide. I would like to see you hang, but knowing General Washington, that will not happen."

Colonel Monroe looked up at Barbara and shouted, "I know that you have something to do with that secret weapon that chased my men and me off of the road because I saw the man with you operating it. When I am released, I will find you and hang you!"

Barbara smiled and said, "You have quite an imagination. I think that this war has taken a toll on you—and your mind is playing tricks on you. Where I am going, you will never find me and you will probably be released when this war is ended, and return home in disgrace with your tail between your legs. During your stay, maybe General Washington can find a good physician to treat you for your mental illness." She turned to me and said, "Let us go, Thomas. I have nothing more to say to this despicable man."

General Washington smiled when we said our good-byes. As we were leaving, he said, "Don't get her mad at you, Thomas. She can be a ball of fire."

"I'll try hard not to let that happen, sir."

As we were walking to the car, Barbara kissed me on the cheek and said, "I could never be mad at you, Thomas."

I smiled and thought of her little outburst when I drove my car up the road, blowing the horn.

When we got to the car, we cleaned the brush off and drove back to the barn. After I parked the car in the barn, we walked over and closed the door. I pulled her close, put my arms around her, and kissed her. As Barbara was returning my kisses she said, "Thomas, my love, you are my hero. If it had not been for you, I may have been hanging from a tree." She pushed me away and picked up the spike. "First things first! Put this spike in the hasp, my love."

I took the spike from her hand and jammed it into the hasp. Then we locked in an embrace and kissed again. "Do you think that you could live here in the future with me—and be my wife?"

"Yes. I thought that you might ask me that question, Thomas—and I have given it a great deal of thought. I think that I can live happily with you as a modern woman, and I know that you are the only man that I will ever love."

I pulled her close and we embraced and kissed. As we walked slowly to the house, I asked, "Do you know what I'm going to do tomorrow morning after breakfast?"

"No."

"I'm going to buy six heavy locks and install them at the top, middle, and bottom of both sides of that rear barn door—and throw the keys away. Then I'm going to put up a wall on both sides of that door, so that no one will ever know that it was there."

"That sounds like a wonderful idea. I intend to spend the rest of my life with you, Thomas. If we have children, I do not want them to become curious and open that barn door.

***

DELAWARE INDIANS

I'm a history teacher at a high school in Philadelphia and I love my job. I'm an average American male with brown hair and blue eyes. I'm five foot eleven and my name is John Lawson. I'm twenty-nine years old and still single, but not for very much longer. Let me tell you my story and you will understand why.

My family tree dates back to some of the first English settlers. When I was growing up, my parents always told me stories about my ancestors. They knew a great deal about our family history. I guess that's why I've always been interested in history and became a history teacher.

Last year I started to research and study the history of the Delaware Indians, also known as the *Lenni Lenape*, which means original people. Apparently other tribes knew them as, "Grandfather," meaning older race from which the other tribes had sprung. They seemed to be a very peaceful tribe of Native Americans, before the Europeans came to this continent.

I found very little history on these gentle people before William Penn settled here in 1682. All I found out is that they mainly lived along the Atlantic coast from Massachusetts to Virginia. In my home area, they lived near the banks of the Delaware River in Pennsylvania and New Jersey. They lived off of the land farming, hunting, and fishing.

While I was studying about the Delaware Indians, I thought that it would be great if I could go back in time and see what they were really like. My only wish was to go back in time. I knew that was impossible, but I am a dreamer and love to dream impossible dreams.

At the end of June—after school had left out for the summer—I decided to do some actual field research on the Delaware Indians. One sunny morning, I set out on my mission. My car was parked in the driveway of my townhouse, so I got in and turned on the key. Guess what? It wouldn't start! That wasn't going to stop me. I would call the auto club to tow the car to my mechanic when I returned home at the end of the day. I was determined to leave right away on my quest. Since I live in northeast Philadelphia, I walked to Roosevelt Boulevard and waited for a bus.

My first stop was Penn Treaty Park in Port Richmond. I read the plaque on the spot where William Penn made the treaty with the Great Chief Tamanend. He was a very honest, trustworthy, and peaceful leader of the Delaware Tribe. Tamanend always cooperated with the new settlers, and was always willing to share his people's land.

I left the park and started walking south on Delaware Avenue toward Penn's Landing. I was trying to imagine what it was like when the Native Americans lived here, when suddenly the skies started to become very dark. It looked as if a really bad storm was brewing. I didn't want to get caught in it and I thought it best to call it a day. Since the bus stop was several blocks away, I decided to hail a cab.

It seemed as if out of nowhere that a vintage 1936 Ford yellow cab came rolling down Delaware Avenue. I didn't have a chance to wave to the driver before it stopped right in front of me. The driver rolled down the window. He was wearing a green uniform and green baseball cap. His bright red hair was tucked up under his cap and he looked a bit odd when he looked up at me with his green eyes and asked with a thick Irish accent, "Will ya be needin' a ride?"

"Yes," I answered.

"Well then, lad, ya better be gettin' in before it starts ta pour."

I immediately opened the rear door and sat in the backseat.

"Where would ya be wishin' ta go, lad?"

"That's a good question. If I had a wish that I could go anywhere, I would like to visit with the Delaware Indians before the white settlers came to this country. But knowing that is impossible, I guess that you can take me home."

I was ready to tell him my address when he said, "Well wait a minute, lad! In me cab, wishes come true! I'm goin' ta take ya south of this city where a tribe of the Delaware Indians er livin'."

"You better let me out of this cab. I don't think that you know where you are going. There is no Delaware Indian tribe south of the city. After you pass the airport, you will be in the city of Chester. There haven't been any Delaware Indian tribes living in this area in the last hundred and fifty years."

He stepped on the gas and said, "Ya got a lot ta learn, me lad."

The sky suddenly turned black and a dark fog surrounded the cab.

The driver must have had the accelerator on the floor because we were doing at least ninety miles an hour! I started to panic and shouted, "Slow down!"

The cab driver jammed on the brakes and the cab screeched to a halt. Suddenly it became very bright and the sun reappeared. We were stopped in front of a large oak tree.

The driver said, "I keep fergettin' that tree is there."

I looked around and saw nothing but trees. It looked as if we were in the middle of the woods. "Where are we?"

"Just where ya wished ta be, lad. You'll be seein' some Delaware Indians soon. They'll be wonderin' what all the commotion was about when I stopped me cab."

"You have to be kidding. Let's get out of here! Where are the roads? Where is Delaware Avenue?"

"They don't exist, lad. Yer seven hundred years too early."

"Are you crazy?"

"No, lad. Ya got yer wish! I told ya if ya make a wish in me cab, it would come true. Look, lad, here come some of the tribe members now. We better git out of the cab and say hello."

"I don't see anyone."

"They'll be comin' here soon enough, lad. Just keep lookin' straight ahead at those trees yonder."

As we got out of the cab, I looked in the driver's side and noticed wooden blocks on the pedals, and a child's booster seat in front of the steering wheel.

"I think that I'm having a bad dream. You look like an Irish leprechaun!"

"You said it, lad. I didn't!"

"Do you really mean to tell me that you are a leprechaun?"

"Indeed I am. Me name is James O'Donlon, and I'm at yer service. I've been livin' here in America ever since I was deported fer losin' me pot of gold. Me punishment is grantin' wishes ta people like yerself, lad. It ain't so bad. I kinda like what I'm doin'."

After that explanation, I was speechless. I really thought that I was having a bad dream and I wanted to wake up, so I pinched myself. I looked up when I saw something moving in the woods in front of us. I thought that I was seeing things. A group of Delaware Indians in their native dress was walking toward us!

The young braves had their heads shaved in Mohawk style with their hair sticking straight up, and the older men had long hair. The women had their hair braided in pigtails, and everyone wore buckskin clothing and moccasins.

My driver waved at them and spoke their language as if he knew them. He even called some of the men and women by name. When they got close, he seemed to be explaining to them who I was. Then he turned to me and said, "I know that ya have studied some of their language, lad, so say a few words of greetin' ta them."

I thought for a moment trying to remember the few words that I knew and then I said, "*N'schawussi, N'nanolhand.*"

Everyone looked at each other as if they were sort of puzzled at what I had just said in their language. Then James said something to them and everyone began to laugh.

James turned to me and said, "Lad, ya had better use sign language until ya learn ta speak their language properly. Ya just told them that yer weak, feeble, and lazy."

James told me that we were invited to a feast that evening as honored guests. He explained that the Delaware Indians thought that we were gods because of our white skin. James said that we were welcome to stay as long as we like. He had been to their village before and they knew him. They were always amazed at the magic tricks that he could perform.

"Watch this," said James. "Do ya see that group of young braves walkin' over ta me cab?"

"Yes."

"This always gets em." He waved his finger at them as if to scold them and said something in their language that I assumed meant not to touch. Then he waved his hand and the cab vanished. The braves ran back in our direction as if they were going to be attacked. James started to laugh and, as they passed him, they smiled sheepishly at his scary magic.

"They really like me magic—even though they er afraid of it."

"How do you make all of these things happen?"

"Leprechaun's secret."

"Tell me, James. Am I really here or am I dreaming?"

"Yer really here, John. I can assure ya yer not sleepin'. Ya got yer wish, lad."

"How did you know that my name was John? I didn't tell you my name."

"It's just another leprechaun's secret, John Lawson. I know everything about ya. I heard ya wishin' ta go back in time when ya were at home. Why do ya think that yer car wouldn't start? Do ya really think that I just happened ta drive up when ya needed a cab?"

"I don't know what to think or believe. What you are telling me seems a bit scary. Your magic is one thing, but knowing my personal information is another. You could give that to someone else."

"Don't worry, John. Leprechauns er not allowed ta give away er sell anyone's personal secrets. We would be banished to a horrible place for all eternity. Now come along with me and I'll introduce ya ta the members of the tribe."

"I would really like to live with these people for a while and learn more about them. If I am not dreaming, this will be the best thing that ever happened to me in my entire life."

"Yer not dreamin', John, so follow me ta the village."

In the village, he introduced me to some men that appeared to be waiting for us. Chief Gray Wolf was wearing a beautiful feathered headdress and was a tall, well-built, middle-aged man. The medicine man, Big Eagle was older with long gray hair and he was a little bit shorter than the chief. They both seemed very happy to meet me—even though we could not speak a word in each other's language. The other men in the group were two braves about my age: Red Feather and White Hawk. They seemed to be friendly guys that I might want to hang out with if I could only learn how to speak their language.

Chief Gray Wolf invited all of us into his bark-covered house called a longhouse. We sat on the blanket-covered floor, passed a peace pipe, and talked. I tried to understand some of their words and they tried to figure out mine. Sign language helped us a great deal in breaking down our language barrier, and James acted as my interpreter.

After our meeting, Gray Wolf showed us to a longhouse where James and I were to live while we were staying with the tribe. James told me that Gray Wolf had the house built especially for him, and any of his friends that he wanted to bring with him.

"I've bin here several times, lad. Gray Wolf just loves ta have visitors."

That evening, James and I went to the center of the village where deer meat was being cooked over a huge bonfire. James and I sat next to each other on the ground at the right side of Gray Wolf and Big Eagle. Red Feather and White Hawk sat on their left side. The village women prepared the food and served us venison and sweet potatoes in clay bowls.

I was immediately attracted to one of the young women. She was extremely beautiful! She was about five feet seven inches tall with a perfect figure and long black hair, which she wore in two thick braids draped down her beautifully sculpted back. Her most outstanding feature was her dark brown eyes that seemed as if they could cast a hypnotic spell on any man that dare gaze into them.

"I see ya lookin' at that colleen over there, John. Ya kinda fancy her, don't ya, lad?"

"Yes. Who is she?"

"She's Little Flower, Chief Gray Wolf's daughter. The women here have the right ta pick their own suitor and so far she isn't interested in any man in this tribe. I wish ya luck if yer interested in pursuin her. Ya have a better chance of becomin friends with Red Feather and White Hawk. They er a couple a nice fellas and can teach ya a lot about their customs, how they hunt, and how they provide fer their people."

"I'll take your advice and try to become a friend of Red Feather and White Hawk, but if the opportunity arises, I would also like to have Little Flower as a friend."

James waved his hand at Little Flower, motioning for her to come over. She walked over and James introduced us. I tried to converse with her using sign language. She smiled and used some sign language, trying hard to be polite and talk to me. Then she went on her way helping to distribute the food among her people.

That evening James and I retired to our longhouse. The next morning, I was surprised to see a petite woman that appeared to be in her mid-forties outside with a fire going in a small stone barbeque pit. She was cooking venison and beans for us.

"It's nice of her to cook for us."

"Aye. She's bin assigned ta ya by Chief Gray Wolf ta cook and clean fer ya durin' yer stay, since ya have no woman of yer own. Pretty good idea, I might add."

I walked over to her, waved my right hand toward my nose, and said, "That smells good."

She smiled and seemed to know what I was trying to say. She said something that I didn't understand and then went back to her cooking.

After breakfast, James said, "I'm goin' ta leave ya now, lad." He handed me a little silver whistle and said, "Whenever ya need me, just blow the whistle. I'm the only one that can hear it. If ya want ta leave and go back home, I can return ya ta the day ya left, er any time that ya choose. But ya must remember, lad, that if ya want ta leave, I can't bring ya back again in me cab. I can only grant one wish per rider.

"I took the liberty of packin' yer luggage at yer home before I picked ya up in me cab. You'll find a lot of gifts along with the luggage that ya can give ta these people. They just love gettin' presents." Then he disappeared before I could ask him any questions.

What was I going to do? I thought that he would stay and help me to learn their language so that I could communicate. Now that I was on my own, I would have to figure it out myself. I didn't want to have to blow the whistle until I was ready to go.

Inside the longhouse, I found two of my suitcases neatly packed with my clothing. Next to the suitcases were twelve large cardboard boxes containing about thirty pairs of Nike sneakers in each box. They were of various sizes and colors and each pair was packed in its own individual shoebox. There were sneakers for men, women, and children. I couldn't imagine where a leprechaun with no pot of gold could get the money to buy all of those shoes. The only thing that I could think of is that maybe he and his leprechaun friends had made them—or else it was a leprechaun's secret.

I wanted to start learning the Delaware *Lenni Lenape* language as soon as possible, so I dragged one of the cardboard boxes to Chief Gray Wolf's longhouse. I found him sitting in front of the house talking to Big Eagle, Red Feather, and White Hawk. I picked out one of the shoeboxes and took out a pair of sneakers. I made sign language motions to let them know that I wanted to give each of them a pair as a gift. Within moments, I had all four of them trying on different pairs.

Each of them picked different colors. After they chose a pair of sneakers, they pointed to their feet, looked at me, and said, "*Wanishi*." I knew that must be their word for thank you.

Chief Gray Wolf and Big Eagle started shouting at Red Feather and White Hawk, "*Kschamehella, Kschamehella*." Red Feather and White Hawk started running.

I knew that must be the word for run so I shouted, "Run, run."

Gray Wolf and Big Eagle understood what I was shouting and started yelling, "Run, run." Then I started shouting, "*Kschamehella, Kschamehella*."

We started laughing, including Red Feather and White Hawk. We were all happy that we were breaking the language barrier and learning words in each other's language. Red Feather and White Hawk were pointing at their new sneakers and trying to give me sign language by extending their arms. They were trying to show me how fast that they could run wearing their new shoes. Red Feather and White Hawk must have thought that they were also breaking some sort of speed record for running.

A large crowd gathered around us to see what was happening. I started to hand out the rest of the sneakers to men, women, and children. Each of them would say, "*Wanishi*."

When the box was empty, I motioned to the rest of the people around us and shouted, "Come with me."

I led them to my longhouse and dragged out the remaining boxes and started to hand the sneakers out. I saw Little Flower and motioned for her to come over. I picked out a pretty white pair with pink and blue designs on the sides and handed them to her. She tried them on and they fit perfectly. She smiled and said, "*Wanishi*." Then she took a beautiful necklace made of small shells from around her neck and slipped it over my head and around my neck.

I looked in her eyes and said, "Thank you. You are so beautiful!"

She looked in my eyes and said, "Thank you. You are so beautiful."

I knew that she didn't understand my compliment, but I was falling in love with her. I wanted to learn her language in a hurry so that I could tell her how I felt. I watched Little Flower slowly walk away and casually turning her head to look back at me. I wondered whether she had the same feelings for me.

I got back to work handing out sneakers to the rest of the tribe. The children were thrilled with their new shoes and pranced all around.

When I was almost finished, most of the tribe members—led by Chief Gray Wolf, Big Eagle, Red Feather, and White Hawk—came walking toward me. All of them were carrying something in their hands. Chief Gray Wolf walked up to me and handed me a beautifully carved peace pipe and then stepped back. Big Eagle handed me one of his best walking sticks. Red Feather and White Hawk gave me deerskin pants and shirts. Other tribe members gave me food, clothing, and other gifts. As each person gave me something, I would say *Wanishi*. I think they understood what I was saying and nodded their heads or smiled. It was their custom that when they were given a gift, they would reciprocate by giving a gift to the giver. The women placed the gifts neatly in my longhouse.

After everyone left, I decided to take a walk along the banks of the

Delaware River to see what it looked like before civilization messed it up. As I was walking, I spotted Little Flower skimming stones on top of the water. She didn't see me so I picked up a little flat stone and skimmed it on the water near her. She was startled for a moment and then she turned around. When she saw me, she smiled.

I walked over to her and said, "Hello."

She replied, "Hello," as if she understood.

I tried to ask her with sign language and a few words whether she would like to walk with me on the beach. She understood what I was trying to say and nodded her head.

We walked down the beach for a little while and then she pointed to herself, and then to the grassy bank and said, "*N' lemattachpi.*"

I knew what she meant so I pointed to myself and then to the bank and replied, "I sit."

We sat for a few hours and exchanged words in our own language and sign language. We would each point at a rock or a bird, while saying the word for each object in our own language. We were laughing at each other over our mispronunciation of different words—and we were having fun while learning each other's language.

After a while, we got up and started walking back to the village. I walked with Little Flower back to her father's longhouse. When I left her at the front door, I pointed to the beach, myself, and then to where the sun would be in the sky, and said, "Tomorrow afternoon."

Little Flower smiled, made the same sign gesture, and said, "Tomorrow afternoon."

When I returned to my longhouse, the woman assigned to me was cooking my dinner. I used sign language and asked, "What is your name?"

She understood and replied, "Dancing Water," in her native language, which I did not understand at the time, but would learn later.

I said, "What a pretty name."

She smiled at the compliment even though she didn't understand me. The next morning she had my breakfast of eggs and beans ready.

After I was done eating, I said, "Very good, *Wanishi.*"

She smiled and said something in her own language.

Shortly after breakfast, Red Feather and White Hawk paid me a visit. In sign language, they asked me whether I would like to go fishing with them. Using my own sign language, I let them know that I would be happy to go with them. Soon we were off on one of many fishing and hunting trips.

Over several months, we learned how to speak in each other's language. I started to wear my deerskin clothing and blended in with the members of the tribe. Red Feather and White Hawk became my best friends. Almost every afternoon, I would walk on the beach with Little Flower.

One day when Red Feather, White Hawk, and I were talking privately, I said, "I only wanted to come here to study your people and their customs, but now I must admit that I do have feelings for Little Flower."

White Hawk smiled and said, "My friend, I think that you are hooked like a fish. You will soon be asking Gray Wolf for his daughter." White Hawk looked at Red Feather and they both started laughing.

My walks and talks with Little Flower became even more interesting when we understood each other. One day while we were walking on the beach holding hands, I put my arms around her and kissed her. I didn't even know if kissing was their custom. I found out soon enough, because she put her arms around me and we were soon locked in a passionate embrace.

Little Flower whispered, "*K'daholel.*"

"I love you too, my beautiful Little Flower," I whispered back.

She pulled slightly away out of our embrace, looked at me, and said, "I thought that you didn't know what *K'daholel* meant."

"Honey, in the few months that we have been together, we know each other's language like we had spoken it all of our lives, but I'll bet that you don't know what 'honey' means?"

"What does 'honey' mean?" she asked.

"I'll never tell." I started to run up the beach and she chased me. I let her catch me and then I pulled her close. "It means that you are sweet. I think that you are the sweetest, most wonderful woman that I have ever met—and I want you to be my wife.

She looked at me and smiled. “I want you so much to be my husband that there are no words to describe how I feel.”

I pulled her close and we kissed again. We sat on the grass near the beach and I asked, “Does your tribe have a big wedding ceremony?”

She looked at me quite puzzled and answered my question with a question, “What is a wedding ceremony?”

“It’s when a man and woman exchange wedding vows with the blessing of their parents and the Great Spirit—or God as my people call him. I know that your people believe in the Great Spirit because I have heard them speak of him.”

“It is true that we believe in the Great Spirit, but we do not have a wedding ceremony. If you want me to be your wife, you must bring gifts to my father and tell him that you want me to be your woman.”

“Well, that sounds easy. I’ll get all of my best things together and ask your father tomorrow after I return from the hunt with Red Feather and White Hawk.”

I pulled her close and kissed her. Then we got up and walked back to her father’s longhouse. After we parted, I went back to my longhouse and started to gather things of interest together from my possessions that I thought might be great gifts for Gray Wolf.

The next morning, Red Feather, White Hawk, and I set out on our hunt. It was mid-autumn and we had to get fresh meat to store ahead for the approaching winter.

Red Feather spotted a large buck when we were at the edge of a small stone-and rock-filled dry creek bed. The bank that we were standing on was about fifteen feet high. Common courtesy was to give the man that spotted the animal the first shot with his bow and arrow, so Red Feather moved slowly forward to the very edge of the bank. He strung his arrow and was about to release it when the bank gave way. The arrow went flying into a tree about thirty feet away and Red Feather slid down the bank, landing face down on the rocks below. When he hit the rocks he cried out in pain. White Hawk and I scrambled down the bank to assist him.

I was worried and hoping that he wasn’t injured to badly when I knelt by his side and asked, “Are you in much pain?”

Red Feather moaned and replied, “I hurt inside.”

Blood trickled from his mouth and, when we tried to roll him over on his back, he groaned, “Please don’t move me—it is hard for me to breathe. Leave me here.”

White Hawk said, “If we leave him there, he will die!”

I replied, “If we move him, he may die!”

“What can we do?” White Hawk asked.

“I know what to do!” I answered.

I blew the whistle that I had hanging around my neck. Within an instant, James appeared. When he saw Red Feather, he exclaimed, “May the saints preserve us? What has happened ta him?”

“He fell on the rocks and we can’t move him,” I answered. “We need your help, James.”

“Aye, indeed ya do. Stand back, lads, I’ll take care of movin’ him.”

James waved his right hand and his cab appeared up on the bank about twenty feet away. The back door swung open and the entire cab stretched so that the seats were longer. Then he moved his left hand and Red Feather floated in the air as if he was on a mattress. James pointed with his right hand and Red Feather floated gently onto the seat. James said, “Quick! Get in me cab, lads.”

White Hawk and I hopped in the front seat and we were instantly at Gray Wolf’s longhouse. Big Eagle and Gray Wolf were talking near the house when we arrived. We got out of the cab and White Hawk told them what had happened. Little Flower came out of the longhouse as we were talking and stood next to her father. She seemed concerned about Red Feather’s injuries and had a worried look on her face.

Big Eagle took a look at Red Feather and shook his head sadly. He said, “I have seen injuries like this before. There is nothing that I can do. He must have medicine more powerful than mine or he will die.”

I said, “There is medicine that can help Red Feather in the land that I came from.” Not wanting to offend Big Eagle, I asked, “Can I have your permission to take him with me?”

Big Eagle looked at Gray Wolf and said, “If you can help him, go quickly!”

James said, “Ya must understand John, I can bring Red Feather back in me cab once he is healed, but you must stay behind. Ya don't have any more wishes left, lad!"

"I know. Red Feather is my friend. If we don't go, he will die!"

Little Flower asked, "Please take me with you, John."

"I can't take you. You could never get used to living in the land that I came from. As soon as Red Feather is well, I must send him back. It would be too hard for even him to live in my world."

She started to cry. "I love you, John."

I pulled her close and put my arms around her. I kissed her beautiful tear-stained face and said, "I will love you and remember you for the rest of my life."

"I will wait for you. Maybe the Great Spirit will be kind to us and send you back to me."

I kissed her one last time and got into the cab next to James. "Let's go to Northeast Hospital in Philadelphia—they have a trauma center."

We went through the black fog again and were in front of the hospital emergency room in a flash. When I ran inside, I couldn't understand why everyone was staring at me until I remembered that I was dressed in Native American clothing.

I ran up to a doctor and said, "Please, you have to help my friend! I think he's bleeding internally."

The doctor followed me outside where I found Red Feather unconscious and laying on a gurney. The cab—and James—had disappeared.

The doctor took one look at him and said, "Help me wheel him inside. What happened to him?"

"He fell about fifteen feet onto some rocks."

The doctor told me to go to the waiting room and he promised to let me know how my friend was doing. I waited for a half an hour before the doctor came in. He asked me why we were dressed in Native American clothing, and I told him that we were at a tribal picnic when my friend was hurt.

"We had a hard time trying to figure out what your friend was talking about. He was speaking in another language. We were ready to have you come up to the operating room when Dr. Brown came in. He's a Native American and speaks your friend's language."

"My friend speaks English. He is probably delirious. He does live on a reservation out West and is just visiting. They usually speak in their native tongue back home."

The doctor seemed to accept my explanation and told me that someone would be back to talk to me when my friend was out of danger.

In the waiting room, people would come and go, but each would ask why I was dressed in a Native American costume. I told them the story about my friend and the picnic. For almost five hours I worried about Red Feather and prayed that he would be alright.

Finally a man walked in and said, "Hi, I'm Dr. Brown.

"I'm John Lawson. How is my friend?"

"Your friend had some internal injuries, but he will recover. Right now, he is still asleep in the recovery room. I need some information about your friend—and don't give me the story about the picnic. I can speak his language. I would also like to know where the two of you got those ancient clothes. They look like they are in mint condition."

"Dr. Brown, do you have a private office where we can talk?"

"Yes."

Once inside the office, I told him my story. When I was finished, he asked, "Do you expect me to believe that tale?"

"No. I guess that I'll just have to prove it."

I put the whistle in my mouth and blew it. In an instant, James was standing in the room.

"James O'Donlon at yer service, sir."

"Do you believe me now?"

When Dr. Brown regained his composure, he replied, "If this is the real thing, can you take me to the village?"

"Red Feather must be completely healed before I grant ya one wish in me cab."

"I guarantee it," said Dr. Brown. "You see, I have a special interest in Red Feather. My ancestors were from the Delaware *Lenni Lenape* tribe. If he should die, I may not exist!"

"Aye. That might be a bit of a problem. John has had a long day and has his own problems, as ya know, so let me drive him back ta his house. We'll talk about yer trip ta the village later when Red Feather has recovered."

Dr. Brown said, "Red Feather should be waking up by now. I think it would be a good idea if you and John are the first ones that he sees because his surroundings will seem strange to him."

"Let's hurry," said James.

When we reached the recovery room, Red Feather was just waking. Dr. Brown pulled the curtains around his bed so that Red Feather could not see the rest of the room. When Red Feather started to wake up and look around I said, "Please rest, my friend. Don't try to get up or you may hurt yourself."

"All right," he answered. "Where am I, John—and who is that man standing next to James?"

"You are in the land where I came from. I spoke of it many times to you."

"You told me that you would never go back to your land—and if you did, you could not return to my village. You said that you would have to leave us forever! Why are we here, John?"

"The man standing next to James is a great medicine man. He is like Big Eagle," I answered. "His name is Dr. Brown. He is one of the people that helped to heal you. You would have died if I didn't bring you here. When you are well, you can return to your village and Dr. Brown may want to return with you."

"But you cannot return to our village," said Red Feather. "You should have left me to die! You can never return to Little Flower! You have given up so much for me."

"I didn't have time to think about it. At the time, your life was more important to me."

Dr. Brown said, "John, we must move Red Feather to a private room."

"All right, doctor," I replied. I told Red Feather not to be afraid of the things that he would see on the way to his room, and that it would be all right for him to close his eyes.

Red Feather said, "John, if you are not afraid of this place, I will not be afraid."

He looked around in amazement on the way to his room, but he said nothing. When we got him into his room, he said, "This place is different, but I am not afraid of it." He pointed to the television mounted on a wall bracket and asked, "What is that?"

I answered, "That is a television. I'll show you how it works later. Get some sleep now. You have had a hard day."

"All right, my friend." He drifted off to sleep.

I asked Dr. Brown if it would be all right if I stayed with Red Feather that evening. He told me that I could stay as long as I like, and that he would have something sent up for me to eat. I thanked Dr. Brown and James for their help. I told James that I was going to stay all night. I wanted to be there when Red Feather woke up.

As they were leaving, James said, "Just blow the whistle when ya want ta go home and I'll take ya there, lad."

The dietician brought me up some dinner about twenty minutes later. She stared at me, but didn't say anything. After I ate, I fell asleep in a comfortable padded chair next to Red Feather's bed.

The next morning, we both awoke at the same time. The same dietician came in with breakfast for both of us and said, "That is a great costume that you are wearing."

"Thank you for the compliment," I replied.

The floor nurse came in to check Red Feather's temperature and pulse, and said practically the same thing. I also thanked her for the compliment.

I stayed with Red Feather most of the day. I showed him how to work the buttons on the bed to raise and lower it, and put it in a comfortable position, so that he wouldn't be in much pain. I taught him how to work the television remote. He said, "Everything that I am watching is some kind of magic, it cannot be real."

I replied, "You will be very surprised when I take you to my house to recuperate. On the way there, you will see many of the things that you are watching on the television."

He looked at me with a puzzled expression and didn't say a word.

"The food that they give me to eat is very mushy. Don't they have any deer meat or something more solid that I can chew?"

"They have to feed you soft food for a few days until you start to heal. Solid food might harm you." He seemed to understand and didn't complain anymore. "I am going home so please don't to try to get out of bed unless the nurse helps you." I handed him a little pad connected to the wire next to his bed. "Just press the button to call the nurse if you need her and she will come to help you. Don't worry, my friend, I will return tomorrow."

"I will be all right, John, and thank you for being such a good friend."

Once I was outside, I blew my silver whistle and instantly James was there in his cab.

James asked, "How er ya feelin' now, lad?"

"Tired. Why is it so hot? When we left the village, it was autumn. I lost track of the months, but I know that it wasn't this hot. Are we having a heat wave?"

"Aye, lad. We er havin' a bit of heat wave, but I brought ya back ta the day after ya left so the neighbors wouldn't be so newsy. Ya have the whole summer ta take care of Red Feather before ya return ta work at the school."

I started to think about all that had happened. "If there were only some other way that I could have saved Red Feather's life, I would have done it, but getting him here was my only choice. I had to sacrifice my future with Little Flower and now I have nothing left—only the memories of what could have been a wonderful life. I'm glad that I'll have some time to be with my friend before he leaves. Maybe I can teach him some things about our culture before he has to go home."

On the way home, James said, "I took a few thousand dollars out of yer account, lad, ta pay for all of the sneakers."

My thoughts were on Little Flower and it didn't seem to matter. "That's all right. I don't care about the money. At least we made everyone in the village happy during my stay. Tell me, James, how did you get the money out of my account?"

"Leprechaun's secret."

When James dropped me off, he said, "I wish there was some way that I could help ya git back ta Little Flower, lad, but the rules er the rules."

I walked in my house feeling really down thinking about Little Flower. I went upstairs, took a much-needed shave and shower, and got into bed. I knew that sleep would help take my depression away temporarily, but anything that helped was a relief.

I went to the hospital to visit with Red Feather every day and would stay until evening. Dr. Brown would stop in several times a day whenever he had the opportunity. He loved to ask questions about his ancestors and their traditions.

About a week later, I met with Dr. Brown at the hospital and he said, "I'm releasing Red Feather from the hospital today. He is well enough to go home with you and I know that you will take good care of him until he fully recuperates. Don't worry about the hospital bill and my services—I will take care of everything."

I replied "Thank you for your generosity."

"I'm just looking at it as travel expense to visit with my ancestors. Can I please have your phone number and address so that I can visit with you and personally check Red Feather to see how he is doing?"

I gave him my phone number and address and said, "You are welcome to come over to my home and visit us anytime."

Dr. Brown and I helped Red Feather into a wheelchair. After we got on the elevator, Red Feather started to panic. When the doors closed, he said, "Why are we locked into this small room?"

"Don't worry—we will be getting off in a moment."

He was startled when the large glass doors at the entrance to the hospital opened automatically. "How do the magic doors know that we are here?"

I tried to explain, hoping that he understood.

Once outside, I blew my whistle and James appeared in his cab. Dr. Brown and I helped Red Feather into the backseat.

After I got in next to Red Feather, James asked, "Shall I take the scenic route er the fast route?"

"I'll let Red Feather decide. Would you like to see the land where I live, Red Feather? You must remember it is the same land that you lived in many moons ago. You will not recognize most of it."

Red Feather answered, "Show it to me. I am not afraid!"

James took us past areas of Neshaminy Creek that Red Feather was familiar with. When he saw all of the houses, roads, and people, he was amazed. "Nothing is the same—everything is gone!" When we got onto Roosevelt Boulevard, the cars and trucks seemed frightening to him, but he didn't say anything.

After arriving at my townhouse, we helped Red Feather inside and sat him in my comfortable recliner in the family room. Then he asked, "Why have your people destroyed the land?"

I answered, "I guess there were too many of us. We needed the land to live on. There are many areas that still look the same as when your people lived here. While you are here, I can take you to those places if you want to see them."

Red Feather seemed disgusted and depressed with the whole idea and didn't say anything.

James said, "As soon as yer well, I'll take ya home where ya will be happy again, Red Feather. I promise ya that, lad. I must leave the two of ya now, but I will be back." Then James disappeared.

Over the few months that Red Feather was recuperating with me—and when he was able to travel for short distances—I drove him to many of the surrounding areas in my car. He was amazed at the high-rise office buildings and said, "The big houses look like they touch the sky." He was totally impressed by the airplanes. At first, he thought that they were giant birds. I took my time and explained everything to him right down to all of the utilities and appliances in my house—and how each of them worked.

Dr. Brown visited with us almost every day. One day, he brought his medical bag and a suitcase. "I've quit my job and sold my house and my car—and everything else that I own. I've decided to go back to live with my ancestors permanently if they will accept me."

"Do you think that is the right thing to do?" I asked. "You've never been there."

"You and Red Feather have told me so much about my ancestors that I really think I will be happy living with them. I have no family here that will miss me—and I know that they can always use an extra medicine man in the village. I can always return with James if the tribe doesn't accept me. Red Feather is healthy enough to return home now, and I'm ready to go with him. All that I am taking with me is my medical bag and a suitcase full of clothes and gifts."

"Are you leaving now?" I asked.

"Yes, I am—if Red Feather is ready."

"I am ready, but it will hurt me to leave my friend John. He is like my brother."

"Don't let it worry you, my friend. I will always remember you and all of my friends in your village. Please tell Little Flower that I will always love her."

"I will, my friend," said Red Feather.

I blew my whistle, and James was instantly in the room. I said sadly, "It's time to take everyone back to the village, James."

He looked sad and said, "I'm so sorry that I cannot take ya back in me cab. I wish that there was somethin' that I could do ta help ya, lad."

I walked with them to the cab, and Red Feather and I sadly said our good-byes. Dr. Brown and Red Feather got into the cab with James, and they were all gone in an instant. I went back into my townhouse and sat in my lounge chair. I was depressed knowing that I would never see Little Flower again. I wondered if she had thought of me, and what had happened to her so many years ago.

I stayed at home for a few days, not bothering to go outside. I was so depressed that I hardly ate anything. Finally, I decided to take a ride down to the Delaware River to the area where my Native American friends used to live. I drove to the place south of the airport where Little Flower and I used to walk along the beach. It was so built up with commercial buildings that I didn't recognize any of the area. Feeling even more depressed, I went back home.

For the next two weeks, I stayed around the house. When I did go out, it was only to go to the market for food. One day as I was walking into the kitchen to get something for lunch, I heard a noise in the family room. When I walked in to see what it was, James was sitting in my recliner!

"How er ya, lad?" Before I had a chance to answer, he said, "Ya look terrible! What have ya bin doin' ta yerself, lad?"

"Nothing much I'm just trying to survive."

"I have somethin' that'll cheer ya up."

"What could you possibly have in your bag of tricks that could make me feel better?"

"A trip back ta where ya want ta be … with Little Flower."

"I thought that you couldn't take me back in your cab."

"That's right. But remember when I was doin' all that wishin' that I could take ya back ta Little Flower?"

"Yes."

"Well. Another leprechaun heard me wishes, and when a leprechaun makes a wish from the bottom of his heart with feelin' and another leprechaun hears it, he can grant the wish if he deems it worthwhile. Well, me own cousin Dennis O'Boyle heard me wish, and he would grant it. So, lad, whenever yer ready, we can leave."

I was overjoyed. All of a sudden, my depression was completely gone and I was happy again. "James, you are the best leprechaun friend anyone could ever have."

"Don't mention it. I don't want ta git a swelled head. When do ya want ta leave, John?"

"Just as soon as I can sell my house, my car, and everything else that I own. I was going to let you sell everything for me before Red Feather's accident, but now I have a special need for the money."

"Why would ya be needin all that money, John?"

"It's my secret. Would you do me a favor and tell Little Flower that I am returning?"

"I already told the poor girl as soon as I found out that ya could return. Ya should have seen her. She looked awful! I couldn't let the poor girl suffer. She's as happy as a lark now, and she's got herself all spruced up waitin' fer ya ta come back, lad, so hurry it up and close yer affairs."

"I'm starting today!"

"Good. When yer ready, blow the whistle and I'll be back with me Cousin, Dennis." Then he disappeared without saying another word.

It took two months to sell everything that I owned. I gave notice to my principal that I was leaving my job. I told him that I was going to a Native American village to teach the children. He shook my hand and wished me luck as I walked out of the school door for the last time.

I went to my bank and put all of my money into a cashier's check made out to James O'Donlon. I walked out to the bank parking lot carrying a suitcase full of gifts for Gray Wolf so that he would give me his daughter for my wife.

I blew my whistle and instantly a small yellow shuttle bus appeared. The door opened and James got out with the bus driver following close behind him. The driver was as short as James. He had bright red hair, wore a green suit, and had a green bus drivers' hat on his head. His facial features were similar to James and they looked like they were related.

"This is me cousin, Dennis O'Boyle. Now hurry and git in the bus, lad! We must be off before someone takes notice ta us standin' here."

"Wait one second, James!" I handed the check to him. "Here is a check made out to you for all that you have done for me."

When James looked at the amount, he said, "Great God in heaven, John you've made a big mistake. You've written the wrong amount on this check."

"It's no mistake. I have no need for money. Where I'm going, it's useless. You may be able to put it to good use."

James was overwhelmed and his eyes filled with tears. "This is a most generous gift, John. If anyone gives a gift ta a leprechaun out of generosity, it means that if the leprechaun is bein' punished fer any reason, the punishment is revoked because of the good deed done by a human. John, I can return home ta Ireland and me family. Me pot of gold will find me no matter where I buried it in me homeland. It's no longer lost! It'll be a glowin' in the spot where I buried it so that only I can see it. If ever ya need anything, I will git it fer ya. I am truly beholden ta ya. Thank ya from the bottom of me heart, John."

"Right now, the only thing that I need is to get back to Little Flower."

"Let's not stand here ferever," said Dennis. "Git on me bus and let's git out a here."

"Aye," said James. "Let's git movin'—everyone git on the bus."

Dennis put it in gear and stepped on the gas, and we were on our way into the black fog again. The fog cleared as it had on my first trip and the sun was shining. When we stopped near the village and got off of the bus, I said to James, "It's a little chilly isn't it?"

"I had ta drop ya off a month later than I dropped off Dr. Brown so that everyone in the village could git used ta him. Everyone loves him, including the medicine man, Big Eagle. Ya need ta dress warm John er you'll catch yer death of cold."

James walked back on the bus and pulled out my winter jacket from behind a seat. He came back out and handed it to me. "Put this on. I brought some of yer winter clothin' ta yer longhouse. You'll be needin' them until Little Flower makes ya some heavy winter clothin' out of bearskin."

In the village, everyone was waiting for us as if it was some kind of a reception. Gray Wolf, Big Eagle, Red Feather, White Hawk, Dr. Brown, and the other villagers were waving their arms and cheering for me. I was their returning hero. Little Flower came out of her father's longhouse and ran toward me. I dropped my suitcase and ran to meet her. When we met, we locked in a tight embrace, kissing each other passionately.

"I thought that you would never come back to me, John."

"I will never leave you again, my love. I brought a suitcase with some really great gifts for your father. He's going to love the fishing equipment. Let's not waste any more time. I'll ask him if I can have you for my wife right now—if you want me."

"I want to be your wife more than anything that I have ever desired in my life. I'll stand next to you when you ask my father if we can be together."

I walked back, picked up the suitcase and Little Flower and I walked up to her father.

"Gray Wolf, I have brought you many gifts in this suitcase. It is all yours to keep. I am giving them to you because I love your daughter, Little Flower, and I would like your permission to take her to be my wife."

Gray Wolf looked at me sternly as if he was going to say no. When he couldn't hold the stern look any longer, he smiled and almost broke into laughter. "You thought that I was going to say no. I could tell by the look on your face, John Lawson. I would give you my daughter, Little Flower, even if you did not bring me any gifts. We will have a celebration today for you and my daughter—for now I have you as my new son."

I turned to Little Flower and said, "In front of all of these witnesses, I take you, Little Flower, to be my wife. I will love you and honor you as long as we both shall live."

"They are such beautiful words, John Lawson. I will also love you and honor you as long as we both shall live."

James and Dennis, who were standing near us with their hats in their hands and big smiles on their faces, chimed in.

"What God has joined tagether—let no man put asunder."

***

JOURNEY TO ATLANTIS

I'm writing my story and hope that one day you who have found it will copy it into your language, so that others may know what happened. My name is Osage. It used to be George Lester, but that was many years ago.

I was twenty-five years old when my story began. At that time, I was dating a very attractive woman by the name of Elizabeth Cummings. Our romance had its ups and downs. We would have an argument and then break up for a while, but eventually get back together again.

When we were getting along quite well, we had planned a trip to Bimini Island to relax, unwind, and maybe do some snorkeling. Well, wouldn't you know it; we had an argument the day before we were set to leave. Elizabeth told me to go by myself—so I did! I thought that I might have a better time without her.

I tried my best to enjoy my time alone. I stayed at a first-class hotel and enjoyed the beach and snorkeling. I decided that being alone wasn't what I really wanted out of life, but being with Elizabeth wasn't what I wanted either. I knew that there was someone somewhere that I would eventually find—someone that I would be happy to spend the rest of my life with.

At nine o'clock in the morning on the day before I was to leave, I carried my snorkel equipment to a section of the beach that I had not been on before. As I was walking, I saw a boat rental office. I walked over to the building and asked the man in the office if he had any small boats available.

He had a fourteen-foot fiberglass boat with a twenty-five-horse outboard motor. He asked where I wanted to go, and I told him that I wanted to go a little distance offshore to snorkel.

He pointed out an area just at the horizon where there might be some good snorkeling. Someone told him that there was some kind of rock formation in that area, and that it might be the ruins of Atlantis. He told me not to go beyond visual contact with the beach—even though the boat was equipped with a compass—because I was not familiar with the area.

I paid him with my credit card and thanked him for his information. Then I went down to the dock, got into the boat, and sat in the driver's seat. The boat had a steering wheel mounted on the right front panel. The throttle was mounted on the right side of the steering wheel, and the electric starting button and compass were on the left. It all seemed easy enough to operate. I started the outboard motor and untied the lines. After I threw them on the dock, I was on my way. The compass was reading that I was heading northeast.

When I was far enough out into the Atlantic Ocean, I shut off the motor and dropped the anchor. The anchor line wasn't very long but it must have caught on something, because the boat didn't seem to be moving. After tugging on the rope a few times, I was sure that the anchor was secure. I could see the shoreline and it appeared to be fixed in one spot, so I put on my equipment and jumped into the water.

I started looking for the rock formation that the rental agent had spoken of. I spotted some rocks about ten feet from the boat, but they were about fifty feet down. The formation looked as if it could have been a building, but without scuba equipment, I couldn't really tell. I was also skeptical about it being the ruins of Atlantis. There were some different varieties of fish in the area, but not many. I had seen more fish near the beach where I had been snorkeling all week.

After a while, I decided that I had enough snorkeling and climbed back into the boat. I was looking at the shoreline and could see my hotel on the horizon. I started the motor and turned around away from the shoreline to pull up the anchor. I was ready to push the throttle in forward and head back to the beach, but the beach had suddenly disappeared! A thick blanket of fog had engulfed the entire area surrounding the boat. I couldn't tell the sky from the water!

I started to panic and my heart pounded. I took a deep breath and calmed myself down. I had never panicked and I was determined not to start now. I looked at the compass and turned the boat to the southwest and headed slowly in that direction. My best bet was to follow the compass reading because I knew that I would eventually get to the beach and possibly break out of the fog.

I pushed the throttle forward and picked up speed still heading southwest, but suddenly the compass started to spin! It kept spinning so I brought the boat to a full stop. Still trying to remain in control of my situation, I shut off the motor and dropped the anchor. It ran out to the end of the line, but the anchor didn't catch on anything. There seemed to be no bottom, so I left the anchor stay out in the event that it would snag on something under the water.

I decided to wait until the fog lifted before I started the motor again. I didn't want to use up the gasoline because there was no way of knowing how far or where I was drifting. The compass was another problem because it was still spinning. I was wondering why the compass was spinning—it had been working fine until now.

Suddenly out of the fog I saw an ancient ship sailing toward my boat. The sails were filled with wind even though there wasn't a hint of a breeze. It was coming full speed in my direction, and it was going to hit me! I frantically started the motor and pushed the throttle full forward to get out of the ship's way. After I got out of the way, I turned my boat around and was going to yell for help. I changed my mind in a hurry, because that's when I saw the name printed on the bow of the ship. It was the *Flying Dutchman*! The ghost ship that had been lost in the Devil's Triangle hundreds of years ago!

That's when I knew that I had a serious problem. I knew about all of the reports of boats and airplanes that had been lost in the Devil's Triangle—never to be seen again. Was this to be my fate? Was I to be lost at sea—never to be heard from again?

I was ready to shut off the motor when I saw the *Flying Dutchman* heading in my direction again. It was deliberately trying to ram into me. I couldn't see anyone on the vessel. Who was guiding it? I pushed the throttle forward again and raced away from the area, hoping that I wasn't going in circles in the thick fog. Why was the *Flying Dutchman* pursuing me? Did it need crewmembers for its ghostly voyage? I had no intention of being one of the crew so I kept going at full throttle, hoping that the ship wouldn't find me again.

It seemed as if I had traveled for miles before I felt safe enough to stop. I looked around and didn't see the ship so I shut off the motor and tried to keep my composure. I thought that if I sat calmly and waited, that the fog would lift and somehow I would get out of the situation. The anchor was still out and not digging into anything, but maybe—with a little luck—it would catch on something. I prayed to God that it would!

I had been drifting for almost two hours when I looked at my waterproof diving watch. It was stopped at twelve o'clock! I tried to make it work, but it was useless. I knew that it was about two o'clock and the sun should be high in the sky, but everything looked gray in the fog.

Suddenly the boat lurched and came to a stop. The anchor had caught on something! I pulled on the anchor line and it was holding fast. Then the fog started to lift. I could make out a sandy beach about a hundred yards in front of me. The water was calm and there were no waves.

I pushed the button to start the motor, but nothing happened. I wasn't getting any spark from the battery. I tried to pull-start the motor manually using the starting cord, but nothing happened. The motor still wouldn't start. There was an oar setting in a bracket on the inside panel of the boat, so I lifted it out. I pulled up the anchor and paddled my way to the beach, running the boat up on the sand.

I got out and looked around. The fog had lifted almost completely and I could see the ocean. I had drifted into an inlet. There were trees and freshly plowed fields about a half a mile from where I was standing. I was confused because it didn't look anything like Bimini Island. I had started walking toward some buildings in the distance when someone started speaking to me in a language that I couldn't understand. The voice was coming from above—almost directly over my head. I saw a man with long black hair, dark brown eyes, and tan skin. He was dressed in clothing that I had seen in an old movie about Egypt and Cleopatra—and he was floating in the air on a large carpet!

He floated to the ground, got up off of the carpet, and motioned for me to get on the carpet with him.

I shook my head and said, "No! I'm not getting on your carpet. If you want to lead me to that town, I will walk on the ground and follow you. How do you make that carpet fly?"

He didn't answer my question and just looked at me with sort of a puzzled expression. It seemed as if he couldn't understand what I was saying. Then he turned away and stared at the buildings in the distance for a moment as if in a trance, and then he turned in my direction again. He motioned with his hand as if he meant for me to wait a moment, and then he looked back at the buildings again. I decided to look at the buildings to see what he was expecting to happen next. I thought that maybe he was going to make them disappear.

In a few moments, I saw another man flying on another large carpet coming in our direction. He floated to the ground and stood up. He was an older man with long, black hair streaked with gray. His skin was also tan and he was wearing Egyptian clothing.

In perfect English, he said, "Do not be afraid to get on the carpet. We use them to travel on more comfortably. We can levitate and move about our land with them—or without them. Sometimes we use telepathy to communicate—especially over long distances. That is how I knew that you were here. The man standing next to you is Seth. He thought that you spoke English and sent for me since he does not understand your language. We usually speak in our own language and only use telepathy when we feel that it is necessary, so don't be afraid—you won't hear voices in your head."

He handed me some clothing that was lying on the carpet and said, "Put these on. They will protect you from the sun. My name is Baruti, which means teacher in your language. What is your name and where do you travel from?"

As I was putting on the clothing, I answered, "My name is George Lester and I came from Bimini Island."

"Where is Bimini Island?"

"It can't be very far from here. It's probably just over the horizon. I couldn't have drifted very far away from it."

"I do not know of an island anywhere nearby. Is that where you live?"

"No. I live in a city named Philadelphia. It's in the United States."

"I have heard of the United States. Others that came here before you and taught me your language have spoken of it. They said that it was in the West and had many large cities and high buildings. There is a large landmass in the West across a small ocean and many tribes of native people with red skin live there. They are farmers and hunters, but the things that they described do not exist."

"That's impossible! It's heavily populated! There are large cities and millions of people live there!"

"That is what the others that came here before you said, but the United States that you speak of is not on the western land mass."

"Where am I? What country am I in?"

"You are in Atlantis."

"That's not possible! Atlantis sunk beneath the ocean thousands of years ago."

"The people that came to our shores before you arrived said the same thing, but you are standing on dry ground and you are in Atlantis. Come. Please get on the carpet. Trust me—you will not fall. I am sure that you are in need of food and water. We will go to Tau. It means lion in your language. Our city is also on dry ground so don't worry, you won't get your feet wet."

I obediently got on the carpet next to Baruti. Confused and speechless, I hung on at first as if my life depended on it. After a few moments, I sat up feeling as if I was floating and didn't need the carpet at all. I couldn't help but wonder how these men were able to levitate.

As we approached Tau, I looked down at a busy metropolis with stone buildings of all sizes and shapes. Some of the buildings had rooftop entrances and gardens. There were beautiful shaded parks and outdoor markets.

We gently landed on the pavement of a city street. I was amazed to see that some of the citizens of Tau were moving about the city by floating through the air above us—with or without carpets—while others casually walked on the ground. All of the people looked and dressed like Ancient Egyptians.

I took notice of the buildings because they were similar to the buildings in Ancient Egypt. Massive columns supported many of the stone structures. There were hieroglyphics painted and carved on some of the walls. I was thinking that I would like to stay here for a while to study their culture. If this really was Atlantis, it had to be the greatest find since Columbus discovered America!

The building that we stopped in front of had hieroglyphics painted on the wall above the door. I read them out loud and said, "Welcome to the home of Baruti and Jamila."

"How did you know that this is my home?" Baruti asked.

I answered, "I studied how to read and translate hieroglyphics into English in college. The hieroglyphics above your door lintel are easy to read."

"Can you teach me to translate your written language into ours?"

"Yes. I will teach you if you will teach me your spoken language and how to pronounce it from each of your hieroglyphs."

"I agree. You will be a guest in my home during your stay with us, George Lester."

"Thank you for your kind hospitality, Baruti. Tell me what happened to the other visitors that taught you my language. Can I meet them?"

"They are not here. Some wanted to leave and try to get back to their homes, and others we told to leave because they were evil. I wished none of them any harm and I hope that they returned safely to their homes."

I could feel that he was being honest with me, but I didn't recall anyone returning from the Devil's Triangle. Unless I could find a safe way out, I would be stuck in Atlantis for the rest of my life.

Baruti invited me into his house where he introduced me to his wife, Jamila. He told me that Jamila means beauty. Her name fit her because she was still a very attractive woman.

Baruti said, "Excuse me for a moment." Then he walked out into the garden. When he returned, the most beautiful woman that I had ever seen was holding on to his arm. She had long black hair and her dark brown eyes looked almost black. Her skin was tan and she had a perfect figure. "George Lester, I want you to meet my daughter, Neferet Siti."

I said, "It is an honor to meet you and your family."

She replied in perfect English, "I am happy to meet you, George Lester. My father has told me that you come from a distant land."

"Yes that's true. I was lost at sea and landed on your beach."

Baruti said, "George Lester, everyone in my home speaks English so you will have no problem communicating with anyone until you decide that it is time for you to leave."

He showed me to my room and said, "There is a pitcher of water on the bedroom table for you to drink. Supper will be served in our dining room in one hour. There is a pool for bathing just down the hallway and one of the servants will have towels and fresh clothing for you."

I thanked him again for his generous hospitality and he was on his way. I filled a clay cup and drank the cool water. I drained the small pitcher before I walked down the hallway to bathe.

The pool looked like one of the Roman baths that I had seen in Europe. The attending servant gave me a towel and fresh clothing. After I changed, I looked into a polished bronze mirror on the wall. Except for my short brown hair and light skin, I looked almost like a native of Atlantis.

I was surprised when I went into the dining room and found that there was a long oblong wooden table and carved wooden chairs with armrests. Up to this point, I wasn't sure if they sat on the floor to eat. I sat across from Neferet Siti and could hardly take my eyes off of her while the servants were bringing in a delicious dinner of roast duck and vegetables.

Our conversation was mainly about our respective countries and cultures. "The people in my country travel almost anywhere in the world by flying in an airplane, riding in a train, bus, or automobile." I explained how the vehicles worked.

Baruti said, "The people of Atlantis can travel anywhere in the world that they desire just by using their powers of levitation. There is no need for any type of mechanical transportation here."

I tried to explain our government and said, "In my country, everyone—whether rich or poor—is equal under our Constitution."

Jamila replied, "Everyone in Atlantis is equal and there are no classes of rich or poor people, because we have no monetary system. We do not buy or sell anything. Everyone has enough food, clothing, and a house to live in. They can even choose their own profession or job. You can be a teacher, builder, servant, or whatever you like, but everyone in Atlantis must do something."

It sounded to me a little bit like Communism, but I didn't want to offend anyone. Instead, I decided that during my stay in Atlantis, I would find out if the people were happy and whether their system really worked.

After dinner, I saw Neferet Siti walking out into the garden. I waited a few moments and then I casually walked into the garden. I saw her sitting on a stone bench. I walked over to her and asked, "May I sit on the bench with you?"

She looked up at me with a smile as if she were reading my mind and answered, "Only if you teach me to translate your written language into my own, like you will be doing with my father."

I replied, "I would be happy to teach you." I was thinking, *you are so beautiful that I would get down on my knees and beg you to let me teach you.*

Neferet Siti looked at me and started to laugh. I couldn't understand why she was laughing. I didn't say anything funny.

When she regained her composure, she said, "George, I know that you think that I am beautiful, but would you really get down on your knees and beg to teach me?"

"That's not fair. You're reading my mind! How can you read my mind?"

"Everyone in Atlantis can read minds. We are telepathic. You are not blocking me out."

"Can you teach me to read minds and block people from reading mine?"

She smiled coyly and replied, "Only if you are good at teaching me the written translations from your language to mine. I could read your mind and learn, but that would not be fair. I would rather have you teach me personally." She laughed again, got up, and walked into the house.

I thought, *Here I am my first day in a continent that doesn't exist and I meet a beautiful woman that I think I could spend the rest of my life with, and she probably thinks that I am a fool.*

The next morning before I started to teach Baruti English, I asked, "Why do you want to learn the written language when everyone here can use telepathy?"

"If for some reason we were unable to communicate one day by using telepathy, we will need to know the written languages. We would rather speak and write—and use telepathy only when we feel that it is necessary." It seemed like a logical explanation so I began teaching him which hieroglyph in his language stood for a letter in the English alphabet. He taught me the sound of each hieroglyph so that I could speak his language.

Each evening, I went through the same teaching method with Nefert Siti. The only difference was that she taught me telepathy and how to block anyone from reading what I was thinking.

I was enjoying my stay in Atlantis with Baruti and Jamila, and especially Neferet Siti. I had been in their home for three months and Baruti and I were becoming very good friends—and I was falling in love with his daughter.

Neferet Siti and I would take walks through the city several times a week. Some of the time she was teaching me how to levitate. When we walked and levitated, we would hold hands. Whenever we thought that no one was watching, I would pull her close and we would kiss—sometimes with a great deal of passion.

Neferet Siti introduced me to many of the citizens and shopkeepers, and I practiced speaking to them in their language. After three months, I was getting really good with the language.

Occasionally I would talk to the house servants when they weren't busy. Their manservant was named Tau—just like the city—which meant lion. I assumed that he got his name because he was very muscular and had tremendous strength. He could levitate almost anything that had to be moved in the house, but he would normally carry most of the heavy furniture. One day as I was talking to him,

I asked, "Why do you carry large pieces of furniture when you can levitate them?"

"I like to build up my muscles because someday I may need strength if levitation doesn't work."

Their maidservant was named Ain, which meant *priceless.* She lived up to her name because she kept the house spotless and was a fantastic cook. Whenever I spoke to Ain, she would tell me that she had a new recipe for the evening meal. I would say, "I can't wait to taste it." This always brought a smile to her face.

One morning, Baruti asked me, "George, would you like to see where we keep the machinery that powers Atlantis?"

"Yes. I had been wondering why I see strange flashes in the sky at night. Is that coming from the machinery?"

"Yes it is. I know that my daughter has taught you telepathy and how to levitate as well. Can you levitate and float without my assistance, George?"

"It's no problem at all. In fact, it seems too easy. I can't understand why I couldn't use telepathy and levitate when I was at home in the United States."

"Come—let us go. All of your questions will be answered very soon." He floated straight up in the air without a carpet.

I followed and, when I was next to him, he pointed his body forward. I did the same and then we floated forward.

"Think faster, George, and you will go faster. If you want to slow down or stop, you must think it. Your mind controls your movement."

I followed his instructions and soon we were traveling at an extremely high speed. I think that we could have passed a jet plane if there was one around. It was amazing; there was no turbulence at all. It was as if we were suspended on a cushion of air.

"Why didn't we use carpets, Baruti?"

"Because they flap and curl and obscure our vision when we travel at high speed. They are convenient at slow speeds when we need to carry something like the clothing that I gave you when we first met at the beach. We usually travel at slow speeds when we have to go long distances because traveling at high speed can become very tiring and we must stop to rest."

After about ten minutes, Baruti said, "We must slow down now."

As we slowed down, I could see a huge pyramid in the distance. It looked similar to the pyramids in Egypt, but it was pristine. There was a large light blinking at the top of the pyramid flashing beams of light in all different directions at the same time. It was lighting up the sky and making it brighter, even though it was a clear day and the sun was shining.

We landed in front of the pyramid and Baruti walked up to a large door at the base. There was a dial built into the door with hieroglyphs engraved into it. He dialed a combination and easily opened the door. The door was made of a strange gray metal much stronger than steel, but it appeared to be as light as a feather. Baruti told me to follow him into the pyramid. Then he closed the door behind us with almost no effort at all and led me down a passageway.

A stream of light ran along the ceiling, looking almost like a stream of water giving off light. When we reached the center of the pyramid, we stopped in an enormous chamber. In the center of the chamber, was a giant stream of light traveling up through a round opening, which ran through the top of the pyramid.

"This stream of light is our main source of energy. It is connected to six other smaller pyramids in our country by the flashing light beams coming from the top. The energy emitted from the pyramids enables us to levitate and be telepathic."

"How does it work?"

"I do not know. Our ancestors built the pyramids and installed the machinery for us. They told us that the machines would work forever as long as no one disturbed them, but we must inspect this main pyramid and all of the other pyramids every three months to make sure that the beams are working properly. We allow no one inside unless accompanied by myself or another elder of our country. Only we can open the pyramid doors to inspect them. Only the elders of Atlantis have the combination to the locks."

"If there was a problem with the machinery, how can it be fixed?"

"Our ancestors told us that if the machinery needed any repairs, we should call them using telepathy and they will come."

"Who were your ancestors?"

"I only know that they came from a star far away in some kind of a disk-like craft. They taught us how to read and write their language. We were taught how to use the energy from the pyramids to levitate, and to use its telepathic power. Then they left and went home to their star."

"That is amazing. I read *Chariots of the Gods* and always wondered if the stories about people coming from other planets in flying saucers were true. Now that I know, I can't tell anyone back home—unless I can levitate back to the United States."

"We cannot levitate from our western shores in a western direction. Something seems to stop us and drive us back, but we can levitate from our eastern shore and return from that direction. We have taken that route many times. You can always leave our country if you want to return home. Sailing ships of commerce come to our shores and trade with us, and they come from many countries. Perhaps one of the ships is returning to a country close to the United States, George."

"Baruti, can you take me to your seaport? I would like to talk to the sailors."

"Yes. We can be there in a few minutes. Are you thinking about going home with them on one of their ships?"

"I thought that I might be able to go home with them for a short visit—just to let my friends and family know that I am all right. Then I will return to Atlantis. I want to stay here and become a teacher. I would like to work with you to help teach the children of Tau how to read and write hieroglyphics and to print them out on papyrus. I know how important it is to you that everyone in Atlantis should be able to read and write if they were to lose the power of telepathy—and the children are the key to your survival in the future.

"You could not have picked a better occupation and I will be happy to work with you and the children. I have always enjoyed teaching and I am honored to have you as a partner in teaching our children."

"There is also another reason that I want to live here in Atlantis. I have fallen in love your daughter, Neferet Siti, and with the permission of you and Jamila, I would like to ask her to be my wife."

Baruti smiled and said, "I was wondering when you would ask that question. My answer is yes, and I am sure that when you ask Jamila that she will also say yes. Over the last few months, we have come to think of you as one of our family. We will be glad to have you as a son. Now let us be off to the seaport."

We arrived at the seaport within a few moments and levitated over ancient ships. They were small, merchant sailing ships! When we levitated down to the docks, I tried to ask some of the sailors what country they came from. None of them could speak English, and I didn't recognize their dialects. All of them sounded as if they were speaking some ancient dead language unknown to me.

I asked Baruti where the merchant ships came from, and he told me that all of them came from the countries to the east. Atlantis had no seaport on its western shores because, as far as he knew, the native population that lived in the landmasses to the west did not have merchant ships.

I sat down on the end of one of the docks to think for a moment, and Baruti sat down next to me. He asked, "What is troubling you, George Lester?"

"I know what has happened to me. I can never return to my home. When I was in the boat lost in the fog and landed on your shores, I was somehow transported thousands of years back in time. That is why you never heard of the United States. My country won't exist for thousands of years. In the distant future where I came from, Atlantis is known as the lost continent. Atlantis sunk beneath the sea from some cataclysmic event—and it is so deep in the ocean that no one has been able to find it."

"When will this catastrophe happen?"

"I don't know. It could happen at any time. You must have an escape plan in order to save your citizens. Is there a safe place far from Atlantis where everyone could go if they had to evacuate the country?"

"There is a place three-days travel from here. We must cross the small ocean and then cross the large landmass to the east, which we call Africana. We have a city under construction near a river that flows from the south to the north."

"I know the river where you are building your city. The name of the river is the Nile, and the land is called Egypt. I think that would be a perfect place to resettle the citizens of Atlantis should a catastrophe occur. The Nile Valley is fertile and good for farming."

"A wise man prophesied many years ago that a man who we would name, 'Osage,' which means loved by God, would come to our shores and warn us of great danger to our country. This man would turn time backward to come to Atlantis and he would live among us and become one of our most respected citizens. The wise man said that we were to build a city near that river and that Osage would lead us there. I believe that God sent you to Atlantis to help us, George Lester. You are the one that the wise man spoke of. You have turned time backward to come to Atlantis. I think that you are Osage!"

"You do me a great honor, but I don't deserve it just because I warned you of something that may not even happen in your lifetime."

"That may be true, but you are a good man and I have a feeling that you will earn your name. From this moment on, you will be known to everyone in Atlantis as Osage!"

As we were returning home, Baruti said, "I am sending a telepathic message to everyone in Atlantis that you are Osage."

Before we even reached his house, everyone that we met was shouting, "Osage is here!" as if I was a retuning hero.

Once we were home, he told Jamila and the servants that they were to call me Osage. He seemed proud of the fact that he believed that I was Osage—and that I wanted to marry his daughter.

Neferet Siti was nowhere to be found, so I asked Jamila, "May I have your permission to marry your daughter, Nefert Siti?"

"I will be happy to have you as my son-in-law, especially since you are Osage—the one that the prophet spoke of many years ago."

I tried in vain to convince her that I might not be the same man, but to no avail.

Neferet Siti walked into the house at that moment and said, "I just came from the market and guess what the people are saying about you, George?"

"That I am, Osage," I replied.

I took Neferet Siti by the hand and started walking into the garden. She said, “You did not have to bring me out here. I will call you Osage if you wish.”

“I don’t care what you call me as long as you call me husband.” I pulled her close and we kissed. “I love you. Will you marry me?”

She looked at me sort of surprised and answered, “Yes, I will marry you, but why didn’t I know that you were going to ask me to be your wife?”

“Because I blocked you out telepathically so that you would be surprised. You didn’t even know that I had asked your parents’ permission.”

“I was surprised. We should go into the house and make arrangements with my parents for our wedding.”

Baruti and Jamila were waiting for us with great big smiles on their faces and arms wide open to embrace both of us.

Baruti and Jamila made all of the wedding arrangements. On our wedding day, Neferet Siti was dressed in white and looked like an Egyptian princess. As we walked from the house with her mother and father escorting us, many of their friends and relatives were waiting. We walked several blocks through the city to a temple. Baruti was on Neferet Siti’s left side and Jamila was on her right. I followed directly behind Neferet Siti. The relatives and friends of the family followed me.

Inside of the temple, a smiling priest dressed in white was waiting for us. The ceremony was similar to the one performed in churches in the United States. We walked up to the altar and Baruti placed Neferet Siti’s hand in mine. Then he and Jamila walked away and stood behind us.

The priest raised his hands and blessed us. He had Neferet Siti extend her left hand out toward him, and I had to extend my right hand. He took a long piece of leather that looked similar to a shoelace and tied our wrists together. He gave us a blessing from the god that created the sun and all living things, and pronounced us husband and wife. We kissed and turned around to be greeted by Neferet Siti’s parents and the guests that had filled the temple.

After the ceremony, the guests carried in two large gold armchairs. Carrying poles were slid through gold rings attached to the armrests. We sat in the chairs and they carried us to a large feast, which I learned later was a normal event after a wedding. The feast was held in a public park with shaded pavilions, stone tables, and benches. Relatives, friends, and neighbors gave the feast. There were various meats and vegetables cooking and roasting in barbeque pits in the center of the park. Everyone brought all kinds of great tasting pastries. There were large clay jugs of wine on every table. All of this was done after every wedding in honor of the bride and groom.

Everyone that attended gave us gifts of furniture, blankets, dishes, bowls, and cookware. When addressing me, they used my new name, Osage. We thanked everyone for the gifts. It was similar in many ways to a modern wedding reception.

Neferet Siti was sitting next to me. I asked, "Where are we going to put all of these gifts?"

"Do not worry, my love. All of the gifts will go in their proper place."

Baruti announced, "My friends, may I have your attention? I want all of you to know that the council of Atlantis has just held a special meeting and sent me a coded telepathic message that only I can receive. They wanted me to make this announcement to you on this special day for my family. The council has just voted unanimously to make Osage an elder of Atlantis."

All of the guests stood up and shouted "Osage, Osage."

Neferet Siti and I stood up as the people were shouting and I held up my hand for silence. When the people were silent, I said, "I thank the council members and all of the citizens of Atlantis for this honor. I came here as a stranger to your country and I intend to be a model citizen and work for you and your families. I will always be ready to help in any way and whenever you need me."

The guests repeated their chants.

Baruti held up his hand for silence again. When the people became quiet, he said, "We must now give the final gift. Let us take the bride and groom to the best gift of all."

All at once, people, furniture, and gifts started levitating! A large woven carpet that looked almost like a Persian rug was brought over by a small group of guests. Baruti, Jamila, Neferet Siti, and I were asked to sit on it. Then we were levitated and led by the guests, following the furniture and gifts for several miles to the edge of a field, and what looked to be a newly constructed stone house. Above the door lintel—written in hieroglyphics was—"Welcome to the home of Osage and Neferet Siti."

I said, "This is unbelievable! Do we receive a free house as a gift?"

Neferet Siti smiled when her father answered, "Everything is free here in Atlantis."

When we landed gently in front of our new home, the guests started carrying and levitating the gifts and furniture into the house, and putting them in their proper place.

After they finished, I picked Neferet Siti up in my arms and said, "This is a custom in my country, my beautiful bride." I carried her across the threshold.

The guests were all congratulating us on the way out of the house. Most of the women were giving us warm hugs. The men were all patting me on the back and saying not to do anything that they would do while being dragged out by their wives and sweethearts. I was thinking that guys haven't changed in thousands of years. Baruti and Jamila were the last to leave after we checked out the house and gardens, and they gave us some ideas on how to decorate.

"If you are hungry, my love, we can go back to the feast."

"The only thing that I am hungry for is your love, my darling."

We kissed and I carried her into the bedroom.

For the next year, we lived like perfect newlyweds. We planted our gardens with all of the beautiful flowers that Neferet Siti loved. Her parents visited with us or we would visit with them.

Whenever any of the citizens of Atlantis had any problems and needed assistance, Baruti or I would help them. I also enjoyed working and assisting Baruti teaching the children. I loved teaching the children because they were always so eager to learn.

We mainly taught the children outdoors unless it was raining. This was because the weather was almost always perfect. It was never too cold and never too hot. I asked Baruti why the weather was so perfect and he told me that the pyramids controlled the temperature and rainfall.

One evening, Neferet Siti and I were sitting on a stone bench in our garden. I had my arm around her and was kissing her on the neck. I was working my way up to her lips when she suddenly pulled away and pointed to the sky. "Look at the sky, Osage! The stars are falling!"

I looked up at the sky and said, "Don't be afraid—it's only a meteor shower. Occasionally they pass by the earth. We usually can't see them in the day time, but at night they are very visible and light up the sky."

"Will they hit the ground?"

"Sometimes one or two may hit the ground. They usually burn up when they hit the earth's atmosphere, and are just small hot rocks when they hit the ground. I have heard of them going through the roof of a house and causing some damage. But don't worry about them; they are too far away to hit our house."

She seemed to have taken comfort in my answer because, when I started kissing her again, she returned my kisses. When the passion started to build, she put her hand in mine and stood up, gently pulling me up. Then she led me into our bedroom.

The next morning, both of us awoke at the same time. I felt a sensation in my head and started rubbing my forehead. I looked at Neferet Siti and she was doing the same thing. I asked, "Did you feel something in your head?"

"Yes. It felt like something was making a buzzing noise. What do you think it was?"

"I don't know."

Then we started getting telepathic messages asking for help. It sounded like a great many voices in panic.

"We must try to reach your father and mother to see if they are all right."

"I'm trying to reach them with telepathy, but they are not responding to my message. There are so many people asking for help that I am not getting through."

"I'm also trying and getting no response. Let's hurry and go to their home. We have to see if your father and mother are in any danger!"

We immediately got dressed and raced to the home of Baruti and Jamila. When we arrived, they were standing in the street in front of their house.

When Baruti saw us, he said, "I just received a telepathic message from one of the elders. Something has happened to one of the pyramids in the north. A small rock fell from the sky and went down through the opening at the top. It has stopped the stream of light and the pyramid is starting to glow as if it is on fire. We are not sure what we should do about it!"

A crowd of people gathered in the streets and I shouted as loud as I could, "Everyone listen to me! All of you must send telepathic messages to all of the people in the area of the damaged pyramid. Tell them to leave their homes and possessions and get as far from the area as quickly as possible for their own safety. We won't know what is happening until we check the main pyramid. Baruti, do you know if there is a control panel anywhere on the main pyramid?"

"There is a box on the outside wall to the right of the main door. Our ancestors instructed us to open it only in an emergency. Only the elders can open it."

"You and I are the only elders close to the main pyramid—so hurry, let's get going! I have to get that box opened! There is no time to waste!"

We kissed Neferet Siti and Jamila good-bye and told them not to follow us. When we arrived at the main pyramid, there was a high-pitched sound coming from an alarm. It was located above a large electrical box on the wall.

Baruti opened the door on the box. Inside were printed symbols for each of the six small pyramids. In the center of each pyramid symbol was a red light and one of them was flashing. There was a switch next to it, but before I could push it to the off position, we heard a loud explosion and the ground started to shake violently. Baruti and I held onto the wall so that the vibration wouldn't knock us to the ground. Then a large mushroom cloud appeared in the far north.

I turned to Baruti and said, "I hope that everyone got out of the area before that explosion."

"I am receiving telepathic messages from the elders that all of the inhabitants have escaped. There are no lives lost and no injuries—thanks to you, Osage. You have saved everyone! Look, the red light has gone out and the alarm has shut off. What should we do now?"

"I don't know. Let's stay near this pyramid for a while and see if anything happens."

We sat on the ground about a hundred yards from the pyramid. I pointed to the flashing light beam at the top and said, "Look at the beams that shoot in the direction of the other pyramids, Baruti. Do you notice anything different?"

"Yes. The beam that travels in the direction of the damaged pyramid has broken off and is turning around. It is traveling back into this pyramid. Why would it travel backward?"

"I have an idea, but I hope that I am wrong! Let's walk over to the pyramid again and check out the switch box."

When we reached the box, I could see that the red light in the middle of each pyramid symbol was blinking occasionally, but the alarm was not going off.

"Baruti, is there another box that might have a switch to shut down the main pyramid?"

"I don't know. I have never seen another box. We only check the pyramids to see if the beams are working properly."

"Can you contact the ancestors on their home star and let them know what is happening?"

"I—and some of the other elders—have tried to contact them in the past to ask them questions about the pyramids, but we never received any response from them."

"Maybe if everyone in Atlantis sends the message at the same time, the ancestors will hear us. Send telepathic messages to all of the elders in every section of the country. Tell them that Osage would like them to gather all of the citizens of Atlantis into large groups. Have them all send the same telepathic message to the heavens for your ancestors or their descendants. Let the message be, 'Atlantis is in danger—send us help!'"

"I will do it now!" replied Baruti. A few minutes later he said, "The elders are gathering the people. They will be sending the message that you gave to me in a few moments."

"Good. I hope and pray that someone receives the message before it is too late. Open the door to the pyramid, Baruti. We have to look for a box that might control this main pyramid and shut it down."

Baruti opened the door and we searched the passageway for

another box, but there was no box to be found. When we reached the main chamber, we could see that the light beam going up through the opening to the top of the pyramid was starting to swell and bulge. It appeared that the beam from the damaged pyramid was feeding back into it.

I said, "Let's look for a valve to shut this beam off. The beam looks like it is going to fill this chamber. If this pyramid blows up, it will cause a chain reaction making the other pyramids explode—and sink Atlantis to the bottom of the ocean."

Each of us went in different directions checking the piping running around the chamber and then Baruti shouted, "There is a valve over here on this large pipe, Osage!"

It was a large wheel-type valve with spokes and a handle to turn it off. Together we started pulling on the large handle to turn it off. We tried to move it clockwise and then counterclockwise, but it wouldn't budge. I said, "Let's look for something that we can use for a lever."

I found a long bar on the floor in a small room nearby. As I was putting it into the spoke of the valve wheel, Baruti shouted, "Hurry, Osage, this chamber is starting to fill with the beam—we must get out of here."

We pulled on the lever with all of our strength—counterclockwise and clockwise. All of a sudden, the wheel snapped off and we both landed on the floor. When we got to our feet, I looked at the broken valve stem to see whether I could do anything else to shut it off.

"We can do no more, Osage! We must get out of here. The chamber is filling with the beam. We will perish if we stay in here any longer."

I knew that I could do nothing more and replied, "All right let's get out of here."

We ran out of the pyramid and closed the door. The alarm was making its shrill noise and all of the red lights in the box were blinking. I said, "We must have the elders evacuate all of the citizens of Atlantis as soon as possible! We have to let them know that, as the source of power from the pyramids weakens, we could lose the power to levitate and use telepathy."

We started sending telepathic messages to all of the elders in

Atlantis. When we knew that they were received and the elders were responding, I said, "Let's get away from here and head for Tau. There isn't much time left!"

When we reached the city, Neferet Siti and Jamila were waiting for us. We held them close and kissed them. Then we told them of the danger at the pyramid and that we had to leave Atlantis at once.

With tears flowing down her cheeks, Jamila said, "I have lived here in Atlantis all of my life. Isn't there anything that can be done to repair the damage?"

"Nothing that we know of," replied Baruti. "Osage has tried to fix the damage. If we had stayed in the pyramid any longer, we would have died."

Neferet Siti sobbed, "Maybe the ancestors will come and we won't have to leave our homes."

I held her close and tried to console her. "I wish that we could wait for them, but we can't take that chance. Baruti, send the message that Osage begs all citizens of Atlantis to leave. We must go to the city that is being built in the east of Africana. We can only hope that if there are any ancestors or their descendants on their home star that they will fix the pyramids so that we can return to Atlantis."

Baruti sent the message and then he said, "The people of Atlantis want to hear from you, Osage. Only you can convince them to evacuate Atlantis!"

"I'll try," I replied. I sent the message telepathically, *"This is Osage speaking to you. Believe me—Atlantis is in danger! We must escape to the city that is being built by some of our citizens in the east of Africana, near the river that runs from the south to the north. Take only food and water with you. Leave all of your possessions behind. There is no time! We must leave Atlantis at once!"*

The elders started sending messages back to me saying that some of the people wanted to go to Africana and wait on the shores closer to Atlantis. Others wanted to follow me to the new city in Africana, while some did not want to leave Atlantis at all.

I sent another message to the people, *"If you want to follow me, I am leaving from Tau in a few moments. Start heading toward the east and we will meet you. I am going to Africana in the east. Leave now and follow me to the new city. To everyone that wants to stay in*

Atlantis. I, Osage, beg you to leave! Your lives are in great danger! If you wait and decide to leave Atlantis after everyone has gone, you may lose your power to levitate!"

I waved my hand and motioned to the crowd surrounding us to follow. Then I shouted, "Follow Baruti and I!" I held onto Neferet Siti's hand, and Baruti held Jamila's hand as we levitated in the direction of the new city in the east.

I looked back and everyone was following us. I heard many telepathic messages being sent from what seemed to be every section of Atlantis. The voices in my head were shouting, *"Follow Osage! Follow Osage!"* I couldn't understand why everyone accepted me as the one that the prophet predicted would lead him or her to safety. Could it be that I was really the Osage that he spoke of? Oh well, there wasn't time to think about it—we had to hurry to get out of danger.

As we were levitating, Baruti asked, "Is it possible for us to lose our ability to levitate?"

"Yes," I said. "If the pyramids blow up, we can also lose our telepathic power. It really doesn't matter. As long as everyone survives, we can deal with that later. We have to keep going as fast as we can—and pray that we make the new city in time!"

After we had traveled over the small ocean and could see the shores of Africana in the east, Baruti said, "We must land here and rest for a while or we will weaken. We have traveled at high speed longer than our normal range and it is not safe to go on."

"Yes. I'm starting to feel a little tired. I know that you told me that it was a three-day journey to the new city, but with thousands of people following us, it may take longer."

"It will take four or five days with so many children and older people following. What else can we do?"

"I guess that we will just move at their pace. We must save them all and pray that God will help us."

We landed on the beach in Africana where we ate and rested. On the horizon, we could see the flashes of light coming from the pyramids—and knew that we still had time.

"Baruti, I don't know how much time we have left. When Atlantis sinks, this beach may be covered with tidal waves. Earthquakes may rock the land that we must travel over to get to the new city. I don't know how much distance we must cover to be out of danger."

"I think that you may be right. As soon as the people have rested for a little while we should move on."

We rested for about four hours and then continued our journey for another four hours before resting again. Each time we stopped, our resting time grew longer and our traveling time grew shorter. We kept Neferet Siti and Jamila close to us for fear of losing our most treasured possession—as did most of the travelers holding their wives, children, mothers, and fathers close to them.

Neferet Siti asked, "Why are you not afraid, Osage?"

"I have fear just like everyone here, but sometimes in extreme danger, an adrenalin rush blocks fear. I guess that I am blocking my fear because my main concern is getting all of these people that are following me to safety. If I show any signs of fear, they will panic. I can't let that happen."

Baruti started to grow anxious and told me that—with our slow progress—it might take five days or more to get to the new city. He suggested that I lead the faster group of people—and he would take the slower group. If the pyramids blew up, at least I could lead some of the people to safety.

"If I am the Osage that the prophet spoke of, I must lead all of the citizens of Atlantis that follow me to the new city—at the pace of the slowest person. They are all putting their trust in me and I can't leave any of them behind!"

"The prophet said that Osage would lead all that followed him to safety. I now truly believe that you are that man—and I will not split the slower groups away from you. I know that you will lead all of us to safety."

In the early dawn of the sixth day of our exodus, Baruti shouted, "Look in the distance ahead, Osage. It is the new city. We have arrived!"

As he spoke, we heard loud booms behind us. We knew that it was coming from Atlantis. I noticed that some of the people seemed to be losing the ability to levitate and were drifting slowly to the ground. The city was only about a mile in front of us, so I gave a telepathic order, *"I want everyone to please land and walk the rest of the way. We are losing the ability to levitate and may fall from the sky and be seriously injured."*

As soon as we were all on the ground, the earth started to shake. People started to panic. They were trying to levitate above the ground, but nothing happened. I knew that they were trying to communicate with telepathy, but that wasn't working either.

I shouted, "Do not panic! Pass the word to follow Baruti and Osage!"

I held Neferet Siti's hand tightly as we walked on the shaking ground toward the city. The workers came running out of the city gates onto the open ground away from any trees. They shouted to us that some of the buildings were collapsing.

I waved and shouted to the citizens of Atlantis to move quickly past me out of the woods and into the open area. I felt like a traffic cop trying to get everyone out in the open area—away from the trees. Baruti stopped just ahead of me and helped me wave the people to safety. We sent Neferet Siti and Jamila ahead about two hundred yards into the vast area of open ground where it was safe. We could see them trying to help us by waving everyone forward deeper onto the open ground.

When everyone was out in the open they sat or laid on the ground where it was safe. The ground shook for almost twenty-four hours and most of the time I was holding Neferet Siti or trying to console her. Baruti was doing the same with Jamila, as were most of the people. They were trying to calm their crying babies and children. Everyone must have thought that the world was coming to an end. I was the only one that knew what was really happening. Atlantis was sinking to the bottom of the Atlantic Ocean!

Almost as abruptly as it started, the rumbling earth stopped its shaking. All of us got up and started walking to the new city. Many of the people looked shell-shocked because they had lost everything and were walking into a new and strange life.

Some buildings had collapsed and others had minor damage, but for the most part the city was still standing.

I said, "Neferet Siti, this is a well-built city. It's practically earthquake proof. All we have to do now is build another house for us—and then we can start having some children."

"Is that all? I will have the children and—since we cannot levitate anymore—you can build the house. It should be amusing watching you."

"I'll have you know, my love, that when I lived in the United States, I was an architect. I designed and built buildings. Would you like a rancher or a split-level?"

"What are they?"

"They are different types of houses made of wood and are easy to build with the right work crew. There are, however, a few problems. My skilled work crew hasn't been born yet, and the materials and tools that I need haven't been invented. I guess you will just have to settle for a traditional stone house."

Neferet Siti started to laugh uncontrollably. When she regained her composure, she said, "The prophet never predicted that Osage would be a fool—and that he would be my husband." She pulled me closer and started kissing me. "I love you despite your faults, my darling. We should start working on making the children first—and then you can build the house for our family?"

"That sounds like a good idea to me," I replied as we started walking to a deserted wooded area outside of the city walls.

The immigrants from Atlantis looked to me for help after they lost their telepathic power and the ability to levitate. I experimented with groups of people and found that if we all concentrated together and pointed our energy at an object, we could levitate and move it. This is how we raised the stones to build our houses and public buildings.

It took several years to complete our city, but when it was finished, we decided to give it the name, "Thabit Tau," which means strong lion. We thought that it was a fitting name because Tau in Atlantis was strong in their memory. The citizens of Atlantis were just as strong to be able to move on and start a new life on a new continent.

We built a monument in the form of a great lion resting on all four paws facing outward, protecting our city and waiting to spring on any would-be attackers. It was designed as a warning that the immigrants from Atlantis were stronger than ever.

Under the ground and near the lion, we built great vaults of stone containing marble chests. In the chests, we put stone tablets and clay jars. On the tablets are carved the stories of many citizens of Atlantis. In the clay jars are papyrus containing more written accounts of our lives. My story will be in one of the chests along with my waterproof diving watch that I could never get to work. I will put it in there as proof that my story is true—and I hope that some archeologist will find it one day in the future.

We engraved a riddle at the base of our lion, and another engraving read, "He who solves the riddle will find our secret vaults with a wealth of information." I know—from my own modern history of the past—that a future pharaoh of Egypt defaced the lion's face and replaced it with his own. You may know the great lion by the name of Sphinx. I hope that the pharaoh did not totally remove our riddle.

I am now writing the final chapter of my life story and I am going to place it in one of the vaults near the great lion. For my wife, Neferet Siti, and I, it has been a wonderful life. Even though we are old, Neferet Siti is as beautiful to me as the day that we first met. We have a son and a daughter, four grandchildren, ten great-grandchildren, and we are expecting three great-great-grandchildren.

I should mention that life for some reason is very long here in Thabit Tau. Neferet Siti and I appear as if we were in our early fifties, but we are both over one hundred and fifty years old. Baruti and Jamila are still alive and look as if they are in their early seventies, but they are really almost two hundred years old. I think it has something to do with the ancestors. They visit us occasionally in their flying saucers and give us packages of food that contain a vitamin supplement from their home planet.

The ancestors look and dress like the people of Atlantis and have extremely long life spans. They have told me that some of the original settlers of Atlantis came from their home planet and taught the inhabitants their language—and how to read and write hieroglyphics. Some fell in love with the inhabitants and they stayed, married, and had children. They have also told me that they heard our telepathic messages for help from Atlantis across the galaxies, but they were too far away to save the continent.

If someday you are walking down the streets in your hometown and happen to see someone that looks Egyptian in modern clothing, it may be one of the ancestors. They tell me that they walk through the streets of the ancient world and speak all languages, but no one notices them. My guess is that they will do the same thing in the future, but that is for you to find out.

***

THE MIRROR

As an antiques dealer, I buy, sell, and refurbish antiques. The name of my business is Paul Granger's Antiques, which happens to be my name. I opened my business about seven years ago right here in New Hope, Pennsylvania, and it really started to grow within the last five years. I have five employees, and my business is large enough now that I can afford to bid on—and purchase—the contents of some very large estates, containing some very old and rare furniture.

I'm telling you about my business because if I didn't deal in antiques, I probably would have never met my beautiful wife, Leona. Let me tell you how Leona and I first met. You may find it unbelievable, and sometimes I can hardly believe it myself, but it really happened.

Three years ago at the beginning of April, I purchased furniture from a very old estate. The house was built in 1860 and was passed down through the family. Many of the pieces in the house were original and made in the 1860s.

Charlie Gordon, who works in my shop in the rear of my building refurbishing furniture, was helping me unload the truck. We gently unloaded a large mirror and sat it on the shop floor. It had a beautiful dark brown exquisitely carved mahogany frame and stood about six feet tall and was thirty-six inches wide. The mirror actually looked as if it was in mint condition.

Charlie said, "Paul, this mirror looks brand new. It looks like it just came out of the box. Are you sure that it's an old piece and not a reproduction?"

"Yes, I'm sure," I answered. "I helped the owner remove it from the attic. It was packed in an old wooden crate. He didn't know what was in the crate so we opened it. The crate was packed with old newspaper that was turning brown and falling apart. The newspapers were dated April 20, 1865, and were wrapped and stuffed around the mirror so that it wouldn't break in shipping. The date and maker's name are engraved on the back of the frame. Take a look."

He read the engraving on the back of frame out loud, "'Thomas Wilson, March 15, 1865.' That is unbelievable—to be so old and to look so new!"

"I know. That's why I'm not going to sell it. I'm going to put in my foyer. It will be a great conversation piece when my friends come over. As soon as we are done unloading the truck, I want to load the mirror back on the truck. Then you and I can take it to my house and hang it on the wall."

We took the mirror to my home in Buckingham, which is only ten minutes from my shop. We hung it gently in my foyer, and when we were finished, we stepped back to see if the mirror was centered properly. "That mirror looks fantastic," said Charlie. "You were right; it really brightens up your foyer."

Another employee, Kathy Wilson, managed the store whenever I was away. After Charlie returned to the shop, I called her and said, "I decided to take off for the weekend and do some odd jobs around the house. If there are any problems, give me a call."

"Don't worry. Have fun doing your housework. I know where to reach you."

While I was cleaning, I saw some fingerprints on my new mirror, so I cleaned them off. I thought that I saw another spot in the middle of the glass. When I started to rub it with the cleaning rag, my hand went right through the glass! I dropped the rag in my excitement, and pulled my hand out so fast that I nearly fell backward on the floor.

I looked at the glass and it wasn't broken, and my cleaning rag wasn't on the floor! I was shaken, but curious. I walked into my living room, which is on the other side of the wall, and the rag wasn't on the floor. Returning to the foyer, I took my pen out of my pocket and put it halfway through the center of the glass. As I pulled it out I noticed that the mirror looked like rippling water. Once the pen was fully out of the mirror, the glass looked solid again.

I needed something larger that I could put through the glass. I had to see if I could retrieve it. I went down to my basement, got a piece of rope, and looked for something that I could tie onto it. The only thing that I could find that was big enough and looked as if it would work was my snow shovel. I tied the rope to the handle of the shovel and went back to the foyer. I pushed the shovel through the center of the mirror and let it drop as I held the end of the rope. I heard it hit a wooden floor on the other side of the mirror. I pulled the rope and the shovel back through the liquid-looking glass and it looked solid again.

I touched different areas of the mirror and they were solid, but when I touched the center, the entire mirror became like liquid again and my hand passed right through. As I put my hand through the mirror, I stepped through onto a wooden floor. Next, I put my head through the mirror and looked around.

I was looking into an antique bedroom! The decorations looked as if they were from the 1860s and they all seemed to match. A window had dark red drapes and the bed had a matching blanket. I saw walls with lighter red gold leaf wallpaper and a gaslight on the wall next to the bureau. The wooden floor was partially covered with a dark red floral carpet. The room was in disarray and I wondered if it was used to store this furniture.

I looked down and saw my cleaning rag. I picked up the rag and, as I did, I looked in the mirror. I was looking at the front of the mirror and it was like liquid again. I couldn't figure out why I wasn't looking at the back of the mirror because I knew that it was a one-sided piece of glass. I quickly retreated to my side of the mirror and pulled the shovel out to answer the puzzling question.

As I was trying to figure out how the mirror worked, my curiosity got the best of me. Was I looking at the storage room of another antique shop? I just had to take a chance and walk through the mirror. I was afraid that the mirror would go solid if I walked through it and I wouldn't be able to return, so I picked up the shovel that was tied to the rope to use as my lifeline. I pushed it through the center of the mirror again, letting it fall to the floor on the other side. The mirror became like liquid again and I walked through it into the room on the other side. I looked back and the mirror was still shimmering like liquid—and the rope was running through the mirror into my foyer. I knew that my lifeline was working and that I could return to the foyer whenever I wanted to leave.

I walked over to the window because I had to know where—and what— this place was. When I looked out, I saw a cobblestone street. People in nineteenth-century clothing were walking on the sidewalks! Some were riding in horse-drawn carriages, while others were on horseback!

I tried to open the door, but it was locked. It had an old-fashioned keyhole-type lock, but there was no key in it. I looked around the room and found a key in the top drawer of the bureau. I put the key into the lock and as I turned it I could feel the lock open. Then I turned the doorknob and slowly opened the door.

I looked out into a long hallway that was decorated almost exactly the same as the room—right down to the gaslights on the walls. I noticed that there were room numbers on about a dozen doors and on my door was the number thirty-seven. It had to be a hotel. I wondered where I was and had to find out.

I put the key in my pocket, walked out of the room, and closed the door behind me. I didn't want to lock the door in the event that I had to make a quick exit from this place. As I was walking down the hallway, I saw an open door. I looked into the room and saw a woman in a 1860s maid's uniform and a white apron. She was making the bed and her back was turned so that she couldn't see me standing there. I didn't want to scare her so I said, "Excuse me. Can you tell me where I am?"

She turned around slightly startled and looked at me. I found myself looking at an extremely beautiful woman. She had light tan skin, green eyes, and her long black hair was wrapped in a bun in back of her head. The dress that she was wearing covered her well past her ankles, but I knew that it was hiding a perfect figure.

"Sir, you are in the National Hotel. Do you realize that you are partially dressed?"

I was wearing jeans, a T-shirt, and sneakers. "I'm sorry. I guess that I'm not in the proper attire for this hotel. I'm having a memory problem. Can you tell me what city I'm in—and what day and date it is?"

She replied, "This is the city of Washington, and it is Monday, April 3, 1865. Why don't you know that?"

Startled by her answer and trying to get my composure, I replied, "My name is Paul Granger and I'm from Pennsylvania. I was at a party last night and someone must have hit me on the head with a bottle." I started rubbing my head and said, "I have a lump right here and I think I have some loss of memory, but it's coming back to me now."

"I'm sorry, sir, I should not have spoken out of turn. I did not wish to offend you. That must have been some wild party. Can I help you?"

"No, I'll be all right. I'll just go back to my room and rest a bit. Before I go, I want you to know that you did not offend me. You have every right to be suspicious of people that seem to be out of the ordinary—with the war still going on. You never know what they are up too. Tell me your name and I'll put in a good word with your employer."

"My name is Leona Johnson, but it isn't necessary to say anything to my employer. They probably wouldn't care anyway. All they care about is that us colored folks do our work and stay out of the way of the customers. But I do thank you for your kind consideration, Mr. Granger."

"You're welcome, Leona, and I hope to see you again. I must be off now." I went up the hallway as fast as I could without running to room thirty-seven. I got inside before Leona could come out of the room that she was cleaning—and shut and locked the door behind me. Picking up the rope and shovel, I went through the mirror and back to my home.

I reclined on my sofa and tried to sort out what had happened. It was hard to believe that the mirror in my foyer was some kind of a time portal that could transport me back in time from Pennsylvania to the National Hotel in Washington. But it really happened!

I couldn't figure out why the portal opened into the National Hotel—or why it was that particular time. I decided to research the hotel and the information that came up on my computer was amazing. I found out that John Wilkes Booth had stayed at the National Hotel shortly before he assassinated Abraham Lincoln at Ford's Theater on April 14, 1865. The National Hotel no longer existed—it had been torn down in the 1930s.

I knew then that my mirror had to have hung on the wall in the National Hotel. But why was the portal opening to that particular time? Was I supposed to save President Lincoln's life? I knew that the answer to my question had to be no! That would change history and the time-space continuum would be disrupted. My question remained unanswered. What was the purpose of the time portal in the mirror?

After dinner, I went to bed early and started thinking about Leona. I was very much attracted to her and I wanted to see her again. I decided to go through the portal the next morning to talk with her again.

In the morning, I put on some casual clothing, hoping that I would look something like the average person in the 1860s. I had some money from that time period in my coin collection, so I put it in my pocket. After breakfast, I put my shovel and rope through the mirror to keep the portal open and I walked through it. After walking into the hotel room, I decided to look in the bureau drawers for some clothing that might be from that time period.

I found a pair of long johns in the middle drawer. I knew that definitely wasn't going to help. In the bottom drawer was a long-sleeve white shirt. It was about my size, so I took off my shirt and put it on. I found a black jacket and a topcoat in a closet and they fit almost perfectly. I didn't find any trousers, but I was wearing black slacks and I thought that no one would notice. I threw my shirt through the portal in the mirror and I was ready to find Leona.

As I was leaving, something caught around my foot and I instinctively pulled it forward. I looked down and saw that it was the rope tied onto the end of my shovel. To my horror, I noticed that I had pulled the end of the rope through the mirror. I panicked, because the mirror was no longer shimmering liquid! How was I going to return home?

I tried to regain my composure. I put my hand up to the center of the mirror. As soon as I touched the glass, it started to shimmer like liquid again. I was able to put my hand through just as easily as I had with my lifeline running through it. I walked through the mirror and I was in my foyer again. I did this several times just to feel secure. On my last trip, I put the shovel and the rope next to my shirt. I went through the mirror and into the hotel room for the last time, reassured that I could get back home whenever I wanted.

I locked the hotel room door behind me and started searching for Leona. I found her making a bed on the second floor. I stood in front of the opened doorway and said, “Good morning, Leona. How are you today?”

“I'm just fine. Thank you, Mr. Granger. How are you feeling today? Is your head still sore?”

“My head is all right and I'm feeling much better. Thank you. I have a couple of questions for you. I hope you won't think that I am being rude.”

“It is Tuesday, the fourth of April, 1865, and I will not think you rude if you cannot remember the date.”

I started to laugh. Regaining my composure, I said, “I'm sorry that I was such a mess yesterday, but that's not what I was going to ask you. I want to know what time you will be done work—and whether I can take you out to dinner.”

“Oh, Mr. Granger, you do me a great honor, but have you looked in a mirror lately. You are a white man and I am a colored woman. Are you sure that you want to be seen with me?”

“Last I checked, white was a color.”

“You know what I'm saying.”

“And you know what I'm asking. So, what will it be?”

“Yes, I would like to have dinner with you, Mr. Granger.”

“Thank you—and from now on please call me Paul. Where do you live?”

“I live in the basement room of this hotel, Paul.”

“What time will you be ready?”

“I will be done at two o'clock. You may come down at three and I will be ready. Just open the door under the steps on the main floor. My room is at the bottom of the basement steps. You will not miss it.”

“I'll be there at three.”

I decided take a walk to see if could find a good restaurant for dinner. Washington looked different than I was used to with all of the people walking, traveling by carriage, and on horseback. I passed several nice restaurants and thought that I would let Leona pick were she wanted to dine. I walked back to the hotel and returned through the mirror to my home.

I knocked on Leona's door at three o'clock. When she opened it, I couldn't believe my eyes. She was wearing an expensive blue and white velvet dress with a matching bonnet and shawl. Leona had to be the most beautiful woman that I had ever seen, including some of the most exotic models on television.

"You look stunning!"

"Thank you. I wanted to look good when I went out with you."

After we left the hotel, I put Leona's arm in mine and we walked to the area where I had seen the restaurants. I said, "Pick whichever restaurant that you would like to dine in."

"There is a restaurant about two blocks down the street that I like. The restaurants that you want to take me to for dinner don't want to serve colored people. They will probably tell us that they have no tables available."

I felt badly that restaurants practiced segregation in the North in the 1860s. I felt like walking into one of them and making a scene, but I didn't want to cause Leona any problems. "Forget them. We won't be wasting our time by walking through their door."

"Paul, maybe I shouldn't be walking so close to you with my arm in yours."

"Why?"

"Have you noticed people are staring at us?"

"I don't care if they stare. I am proud to have you walking with me, so don't pay any attention to ignorant people."

Leona smiled and replied, "All right. You are the boss."

When we arrived at the restaurant, the owner—an elderly Italian gentleman—greeted us. He gave us menus and seated us immediately. I read the menu and said, "They have Italian food here. I like Italian food!"

"I like Italian food and I also like the owner of this restaurant.

He is a very nice man and he caters to everyone—regardless of his or her color."

"I didn't think people in Washington were so prejudiced."

"It depends on where you go in Washington. It may be different where you live."

"It's illegal where I live. No one is allowed to treat anyone like a second-class citizen. It doesn't matter what color or ethnic background you come from, you can work in any profession. Anyone can be a doctor, lawyer, teacher, police officer—or anything else that they want to be. It makes no difference if you are a woman or a man. There is no discrimination allowed."

"It sounds like you live in paradise—and not in Pennsylvania."

"It's not paradise. It's far from it. But that's enough about where I live, tell me about you."

She had been born in Virginia and her parents were slaves. When she was an infant, they escaped from the plantation. Her father had been shot and wounded when someone saw them running from the plantation. They made it across the Potomac River on a barge operated by some white people from the North. They tried to stop the bleeding from her father's wound, but he died before they could get him to a doctor.

After her father was buried, Leona and her mother were taken to live with a white widow by the name of Mrs. Sally Prichard. She lived in a big house just outside of Washington and was quite wealthy. Mrs. Prichard paid Leona's mother to do her cooking, and cleaning.

When Leona was five, her mother died from a fever. Mrs. Prichard raised her as if she were her own daughter. She was sent to the best schools so that she would receive a good education. Mrs. Prichard had grown children that lived in Maryland. When she died, her children thanked Leona for staying with their mother. They gave her twenty dollars and told her that she had to leave because they were selling the property. Leona said, "So here I am in Washington telling you my life story."

"It's not the best of stories, but at least you lived with a woman that cared about you. Tell me with your education. Why are you working as a maid?"

"Because it's a white world, there are not any good jobs for colored people."

I paid for dinner and we walked arm in arm back to the hotel. Before I left Leona in front of her basement room, I pulled her close and kissed her. Leona reciprocated and I felt the passion building.

When we finally broke loose from our embrace, she asked, "What room are you staying in, Paul?"

"I'm not staying here at the hotel. My friend George has a house a few blocks away, and he let me stay in his spare bedroom while I'm visiting Washington. His friend Tom rented a room here in the hotel to have a small surprise birthday party for another friend of his and invited a few people—and that is how I met you."

"I like you, Paul, but there is something mysterious about you."

"I'm just a businessman on vacation. Can we do something tomorrow after you are done work?"

"I would like that very much."

We kissed again and then Leona went in her room. After she closed the door, I walked upstairs and returned to my home.

The next morning, I went to a coin dealer in town and bought some cheap currency from the 1860s. That afternoon, when I walked down the stairs in the National Hotel to meet Leona, I noticed that there was no clerk at the front desk. In fact I didn't remember anyone ever being at the front desk. As Leona and I were passing the desk on the way out of the building, I asked, "Why isn't there ever a clerk on duty at the front desk?"

"Do you see the little brass bell on the counter and the curtain on the little room behind the desk?"

"Yes."

"The clerk is an older white man and his name is Jessie. He works from nine in the morning until nine at night. He also drinks a little bit so he sleeps on a bed in that back room. If someone wants him, they just ring the bell and he will come out."

"I guess that answers my question."

After dinner in another restaurant that Leona knew quite well, we walked around the busy areas of town. We followed basically the same pattern every afternoon.

On Saturday, Leona said, "I don't have to work on Sunday. We could do something tomorrow if you are not busy."

"I always have time for you. I'll rent a carriage and we can take a ride along the Potomac."

"That would be nice. We could leave in the morning and spend the whole day together."

I met Leona at her basement hotel room on Sunday morning. After we walked outside, I started to hail a horse-drawn carriage.

Leona pulled on my arm and said, "It's too expensive for you to rent a cab all day. I know where we can rent a carriage and you can drive it. It is much cheaper."

"I don't know how to drive a carriage."

"Well if you can ride a horse, it should be fairly easy."

"I'll take your word for it. Lead me to the stable." Knowing that I had only ridden a horse about two times in my entire life, I was hoping that I could make her believe that I knew what I was doing.

We walked to the stable and I rented a carriage with a big chestnut horse to pull it. After I helped Leona into the carriage, I climbed in next to her, took the reins, and shouted, "Giddy up." Nothing happened! I looked at Leona and said, "There is something wrong with this horse. He's not moving—he's just standing there."

"Why are you shouting giddy up? Slap him!"

I tried to stretch my arm over the front of the carriage to slap him on the back. "The horse is too far away. I can't reach him."

Leona took the reins out of my hands and said, "Not like that! You have to slap him with the reins. Let me show you. I will drive for a few blocks and then you take over." She showed me how to handle the horse and make turns for the next five or six blocks. "The pedal on the floor is the brake. If you really have to stop fast, push it down hard with your foot and it will stop the wheels from turning."

"The brakes haven't changed much. They are the same on all of the cars that I have driven."

As I took over the reins, Leona asked, "What are cars?"

"Uh, their just a new type of equipment that we use up North."

I was getting used to handling the horse as we leisurely rode along a dirt road near the Potomac River. It was a sunny day and I pulled the horse over into a scenic grove by the river. Since no one was around, I embraced Leona and we kissed passionately.

When we separated slightly, I whispered, "I want you to know that I have never said this to another woman, but I think that I am falling in love with you."

Leona whispered, "I feel the same way about you, Paul, but you need to tell me more about yourself."

As we separated, I asked, "What would you like me to tell you?"

"You are staying with your friend, George, so you don't have to tell me anything—just take me to his house and introduce me to him."

"I can't do that."

"I did not think that you could. I went upstairs as soon as you left last night. I did not hear the front door close. When I looked toward the main stairway, I saw the shadow of a man in the glow of the gaslight making the turn toward the second-floor landing. I followed as fast as I could right up to the third floor. When I reached the top, I heard the door to room thirty-seven close and the key turn in the lock. I knocked on the door and called your name, but no one answered. I went down to my room and got my passkey. Then I went back upstairs and opened the door, but you were not in the room. You must tell me, Paul, are you an agent working for the government?"

"I wish. With my knowledge, I could change history. But it's not that simple. I do live in Pennsylvania, but not the Pennsylvania of 1865. H. G. Wells wrote a book called *The Time Machine*, but he won't be born until 1866, so there is no way that you could have read his book."

"I hope that you are not going to tell me that you travel through time in some kind of a machine."

"Not exactly. Let me tell you how I got here—and please try to believe me." I told her my story and what I did for a living, and how I got to the National Hotel.

When I was finished, she replied, "If you want me to believe a story like that, Paul, you will have to take me through your mirror."

"I know that it's hard for you to believe me, but promise me that you won't tell anyone and I'll take you through the mirror."

"I promise. Take me back to the hotel and show me how your mirror works if you want me to believe you."

On the way back to the stable, Leona sat as far away from me as she could. As we walked back to the hotel, she wouldn't hold my arm. I really didn't blame her because she probably thought that I was insane. She followed me up to room thirty-seven. After we were in the room, she wouldn't let me close the door.

"Leona, while I stand back, gently put your hand through the center of the mirror."

She put her right hand on the center of the glass and nothing happened. I stood as if I was frozen, unable to figure out why the mirror wasn't working.

"The glass is solid, Paul! I trusted you and you have been lying to me."

"It can't be solid or I'll be stuck here for the rest of my life!"

I rushed over to the mirror and put my right hand on the center of the glass. It instantly started to shimmer and my arm went right through up to my shoulder. I was slightly off balance in my excitement thinking that the portal had closed and I almost fell through. Leona was so surprised that she started to scream. I quickly got my balance and pulled my hand out of the mirror. I put my right hand over her mouth to keep her quiet. I kicked the door shut and said, "Please don't be afraid. I'm all right."

I took my hand off of her mouth and held her close while I locked the door. "I don't know why you couldn't do the same thing. I don't know how the mirror works, but if you are not afraid, I will take you through it with me. Do you trust me?"

She kissed me on the cheek. "I trust you and I am sorry that I did not believe you."

"Some of the clothing that I am wearing came from the bureau in this room. If the clothing can pass through the mirror, you should be able to get through by holding onto me. Turn and face me and we'll hold hands"

Slightly trembling, Leona did as I asked. I told her to walk sideways with me toward the mirror—almost as if we were dancing. I put our hands up to the center of the glass and we started to go through. "Keep walking and don't let go of me until I say it's all right." Leona nodded without saying a word.

When we were completely in my foyer and away from the mirror, I said, "You can let go of me now."

She embraced me, looked around my foyer, and said, "I am almost afraid to move."

"I know exactly how you feel. I had similar feelings when I walked through the mirror and into the nineteenth century." I kissed her on the cheek and said, "Welcome to the twenty-first century, my love. Let's go into the family room and sit down so that I can tell you what you are going to see here in my world."

We sat down on the sofa and I held her close while I tried to tell her everything that I could think of that was important and different in the twenty-first century. "If you want to stay for a little while, I'll show you some of my world. We still have some time left before I have to take you back. The time of day hasn't changed—it's only three o'clock."

"I want to see what it is like here on the other side of the mirror."

"All right, I'll show you around my house first."

I took her on the grand tour, showing her the kitchen first and how the appliances worked. She was impressed with the fact that we used gas to work the range, but she couldn't understand how the electric lights worked without gas. The television in the family room really caught her attention. I spent a little time teaching her how to use the remote and change the channels. Leona liked the idea of having the toilet inside of the house instead of using an outdoor privy.

Then we went into my garage. "This is my automobile. Most people, including myself, usually call it a car, which is just another name for the same vehicle."

"What does it do?"

"It will take you wherever you want to go very quickly. The automobile started taking the place of the horse and carriage at the beginning of the twentieth century."

"How does it move?"

"Would you like me to take you for a ride around my neighborhood?"

"Yes."

I pushed the garage door opener button on the wall and the opening door surprised Leona. She grabbed my arm and held on to it. As the door opened, my neighbor was walking his dog in front of my house.

He looked at Leona and said, "I hope I didn't interrupt anything, Paul."

"You didn't interrupt anything, Bill. We were just getting the car out of the garage."

I walked out to the sidewalk and introduced Leona to Bill. He asked why we were dressed in costumes. I told him that we were going to a party and were supposed to wear clothing from the nineteenth century. He was having a birthday party for his wife in a couple of weeks, and asked me to bring Leona. It wasn't going to be anything elaborate and we didn't have to wear costumes. I told him that we loved parties and that we would be happy to attend.

After he left, Leona asked, "Does Bill work around here?"

"No. He's my friend, my neighbor, and my doctor. He lives in the house at the end of my street."

"But he is a colored man!"

"Remember that I told you that it is different here in Pennsylvania?"

"Yes."

"Well, I didn't tell you the whole truth. I couldn't tell you that it is different here in the United States in the twenty-first century. Everyone has equal rights and prejudice is illegal. Now let's get in the car and I'll show you the rest of my neighborhood."

Once Leona was seated, I buckled her in. Leona was startled when I put the car in reverse and backed out of the garage. I pushed the button on the remote that I had clipped on the visor and closed the garage door. She asked me how I was able to close the door. I told her that the unit sends an electronic signal to the control unit on the garage wall. Leona tried to understand what I was telling her, but since she didn't know how electricity worked, it was difficult.

I drove slowly so that Leona could get used to the speed of the car. As we drove around the development, she was amazed at the size of the houses and by all of the automobiles in the driveways.

She asked if all of my neighbors were wealthy. I told her that some of them had a little more money than others did, but it was a middle-class neighborhood.

She had me stop next to the local playground. "Look! The children's swings and seesaws have not changed."

"I think that you are right. Except for the material that they are made of, I guess they have been the same for hundreds of years."

I drove out onto the main highway. She was amazed at all of the traffic and shopping centers. She couldn't get over how the women dressed showing their legs. The styles seemed shocking to her at first, but after a while she got used to them—and even expressed her thoughts on how she would look dressed in twenty-first century clothing.

I drove back to my development. When we pulled up in my driveway, I let her use the remote to open the garage door. Once we were inside, I asked if she would like something to eat before I took her back home. "I'm not a very good cook so I either eat at restaurants or order take-out food from a restaurant. Have you ever had pizza at an Italian restaurant?"

"No. What is pizza?"

"It's a flat tomato pie with cheese on top. I think that you will like it."

After I ordered the pizza, Leona asked, "What is that thing that you were talking into—and who were you talking too?"

"It's called a telephone—or phone—and I forgot to tell you about it. I can speak to anyone in most of the world if I dial his or her phone number, and it will ring if someone is calling me. I just called the Italian restaurant in the shopping center about a mile away. The man on the other end of the phone said that they will deliver the pizza in about twenty minutes."

Leona was amazed when the deliveryman arrived with the pizza about twenty minutes later. I don't think that she really believed that the phone worked. She had three slices of pizza and told me that it was the best Italian food that she had ever eaten.

After we had finished eating, we walked back into the foyer. I was ready to face Leona and hold her hands as we walked through the mirror when she said, "Wait! I want to try going through the glass without your help. Maybe I did something wrong this afternoon."

I knew that, for some reason, the mirror worked only for me and she couldn't get through it without having some kind of contact with me, so to humor her I said, "Just hold onto my right hand when you walk through, and I'll follow you. I don't want to take the chance of losing you."

Leona agreed and put her right hand on the center of the glass as I held onto her left hand. The mirror started to shimmer as her hand passed right through the glass. She looked at me and said, "I think that I was too nervous this afternoon and that is probably why the mirror did not work for me."

When we were on the other side of the mirror, she said, "I knew that the mirror would work for me."

Knowing that she could figure out a way to get through the mirror without my assistance, I replied, "Please don't try going through the mirror without me holding your hand. I have a bad feeling about you going through without me being there."

"Don't worry, Paul, I'll wait for you."

I told her that I was going to buy her some twenty-first century clothing. I said that she could change into them at my house when I picked her up after work on Monday—and that I would like to take her to dinner at one of my favorite restaurants. She was curious to see how it would be to dress like a twenty-first century woman and dine out, so she agreed. Leona told me to meet her at two o'clock instead of three. After we kissed good-bye, I walked back upstairs and through the mirror.

The next morning, I went shopping at a department store. I told the saleslady that I wanted to by some stylish clothing for my wife as a surprise. When she asked me what sizes she wore, I pointed at a female customer and told her that she was about the same size. The saleslady told me that she could give me the approximate sizes and if anything didn't fit, that my wife could bring them back for an exchange.

I bought a light blue dress and matching jacket. Even the shoes and lingerie were light blue. I hoped that everything would fit, and that Leona liked the things that I bought for her. Before I left the store, I picked up a popular perfume that I thought she might like.

When Leona opened her door, she was still dressed in her uniform.

When I asked her why she hadn't changed, she replied, "I want to bathe in your tub instead of getting washed out of the basin in my room. Will that be all right, Paul?"

"Anything that pleases you is all right with me, beautiful lady. Your wish is my command."

"You make me happy, Paul." She kissed me on the cheek and said, "Let's hurry. I can't wait to get into a nice tub of warm water and I want to get out of this city for a while. Everyone in the city seems to have gone wild, shooting guns into the air and shouting. Did you know that the war has ended?"

"Yes. General Lee surrendered yesterday at the Appomattox Court House at 4:30 p.m. I forgot all about it." I told her all about the surrender on the way to room thirty-seven.

Inside my house, I gave Leona the bags of clothing, lingerie, and shoes and told her to put them on after she was done bathing. I led her up to the master bathroom and showed her how to work the tub, shower, and hairdryer, and then I left her to enjoy her bath.

Leona came downstairs an hour later. She had left her long black hair down and looked beautiful in her new clothing. "I haven't felt this clean in a long time. Thank you for the new clothing. How do I look, Paul? Will I pass for a twenty-first century woman?"

"You could fool me. Does everything fit all right? Are the shoes too tight?"

"Everything fits just fine. You did a really good job picking my sizes."

"Maybe we should leave now. I've made reservations for six o'clock at a really great restaurant. Since we have some time before we eat, I want to take you shopping for more clothing. If you want to visit with me occasionally, you will need them. That is if you really want to visit with me."

"There is nothing in the world that I would like better than to visit with you, Paul." She put her arms around me and we kissed.

When we finally separated, I took her by the hand and led her out to my car. I drove back to the department store and the same saleslady waited on us. She said, "Your wife looks absolutely stunning in the clothing you picked out for her."

Leona looked at me without saying a word. I replied, "My wife looks stunning in anything that she wears."

I bought more clothing and another pair of shoes for Leona.

After we left the store she said, "Paul, you should not have told that lady that we were married. If the word gets around, people will look down on you for marrying a woman of color."

"It's different here. Men and women of various races marry all the time. Anyway, I had to tell that lady that we were married. I didn't want her thinking that I was buying the clothing for me."

When Leona finally stopped laughing for a moment she said, "You would look funny wearing my clothing." Her laughter made me laugh. We finally stopped laughing when we got in the car.

When we got to the restaurant, I told the hostess, "Reservations for Paul Granger."

She looked at the list and said, "Just a minute, Mr. Granger. Let me see if your table is ready."

When she walked away, Leona said, "The table is not going to be ready. She is just going to let us stand here. We should leave, Paul. It is just like back home in Washington."

"In the twenty-first century—it's not even like that in Washington. I'll have to take you there someday to prove it to you. The entire country is a totally different place than you are accustomed too."

Just as I finished speaking, the hostess came back and said, "Your table is ready, sir." Then she looked at Leona and asked, "Where did you get that dress? You look beautiful in it, Mrs. Granger."

Leona said, "Thank you." Then she told her the name of the store.

After dinner, we drove home and Leona changed back into her uniform. I followed her back through the mirror, not letting go of her hand until we were on the other side. We walked back to her basement room. After some long kisses, I told her that I would be back at two o'clock on Tuesday, so that she could bathe and change at my house. I went back upstairs and walked through the mirror into my own world. I wished that Leona would live with me permanently.

When I walked through the mirror on Tuesday afternoon, Leona screamed, "Please don't hurt me!"

I quickly opened the door to see her running toward the room.

When she saw me, she ran to my open arms and shouted, "Paul, please help me! They are going to kill me!"

I heard men running up the stairway and one of them was shouting, "Kill her. Cut her throat! She'll be sorry that she ever eavesdropped on me."

I pulled Leona into the room and slammed the door shut. I heard one of the men turning the doorknob as we went through the mirror. We were moving so fast that I tripped on the edge of the frame and we both landed on the floor in my foyer.

She was still crying as I pulled her close to comfort her. "You are safe now. Are you hurt?"

"No," she whispered. "Can they get through the mirror?"

"If they could, they would have been here by now."

"Who was chasing you—and why did they want to kill you?"

"It was Mr. Booth and his friends," she answered. Leona went on to explain that she was cleaning in the lounge area and saw three men sitting around a table in the corner. They apparently didn't see her and she overhead them talking about kidnapping President Lincoln.

She tried to sneak out, but Mister Booth saw her and shouted, "Get that woman! She has heard our plans. Kill her!" Leona said that she started to run up the stairs, hoping that I would be there. While she was running up the stairs, one of the men yelled, "Cut her throat so that she can't talk to anyone!"

We got up and walked into the family room. I told her to rest on the sofa while I made tea. When I came back, I sat next to her and I asked, "Are you feeling better?"

"Yes, thank you, Paul."

"I don't think it's going to be safe for you to return for a couple of weeks. I want you to stay here with me. In fact, Leona, I would like you to stay with me for the rest of our lives. I know it's a little soon and we haven't known each other very long, but I would like you to really get to know me, and one day be my wife. The truth is that I have fallen in love with you."

She looked at me, surprised at my sudden proposal. Then she pulled me close and kissed me. "I fell in love with you, Paul, on the first afternoon that you took me out to dinner. I would love to be your wife if the people here would accept me."

"That's not a problem. All of my relatives, friends, and neighbors will love you."

"There is just one problem, Paul."

My heart started to sink. "What is that?"

"You are holding something back from me, Paul. You did not say one word about President Lincoln. What happened to him? You must know. It has to be written in your history books. Did Mr. Booth kidnap the president?"

"No, he didn't kidnap President Lincoln. The belief is that there may have been a kidnap conspiracy between several top officials in government, and that John Wilkes Booth was part of it. For some reason, the plan was changed a day or two before the kidnapping was to take place. Instead, on April 14, 1865 at ten fifteen p.m., Abraham Lincoln was assassinated in Ford's Theater. The door to his private box was left unguarded and unlocked. John Wilkes Booth snuck up a back stairway and he shot President Lincoln in the back of the head. He died the next morning, never regaining consciousness.

"Booth escaped and—when he was found hiding in a barn by an army search party—he refused to surrender. They wanted him alive, so they set the barn on fire to flush him out without killing him. One of the soldiers disobeyed orders and shot him. When Booth was dragged out of the barn, he was barely alive. He died without naming any accomplices."

"Paul, we can save President Lincoln! We can go through the mirror and save him before Mr. Booth can get to him."

"No we can't! If we did save him, we could change the time-space continuum. Let me explain what would happen. If we were to change history, things in my time would change. Lincoln was a very important man and too many things surrounded him. On the other hand, I think that you were supposed to die! Booth or one of his men was supposed to kill you. When I saved you, nothing happened because you had no close relatives and no children. You can have a new life here and history will remain the same. Stay here with me and don't even think about changing the past."

She seemed stunned and slightly confused, but she accepted everything. "I trust you, Paul." She kissed me on the cheek and said,

"I am going up to take a bath. Can we just order pizza and stay here tonight? I do not feel like going out."

"That will be fine. I'll make up the spare bedroom for you."

Leona came downstairs a few minutes after the pizza was delivered. We had a couple of slices and a cup of tea. Then we cuddled up on the sofa and watched a funny movie that cheered her up.

After the movie, I showed her to the spare bedroom and tucked her in, and then we kissed goodnight. When I got into my bed, I was hoping that Leona could get some sleep after her ordeal.

When I woke up, I could smell bacon and eggs. I went downstairs and Leona was making breakfast. "It's amazing how you figured out how to cook on the range so fast."

"After you showed me how it worked, it was easy to figure out how to cook on it. It is so much better and faster than cooking on a wood-burning stove. I even made you toast in that machine that you call a toaster." She sat two plates of scrambled eggs and bacon and two cups of tea on the kitchen table. "I hope that you like my cooking."

We sat down at the table and started eating. I said, "These are the best eggs and bacon that I have ever had in my entire life!"

"You are the biggest storyteller that I have ever heard in my life. After we are done eating, you can wash the dishes."

"That's not a problem. Just wait until I show you how the garbage disposal and dishwasher work."

After breakfast, Leona was amazed when I showed her how those appliances worked. I told her to get dressed because I was going to take her to my store and introduce her to my employees, and then show her around New Hope.

When we got to the store, my employees were totally impressed with Leona. Kathy told Leona that she didn't think that I was ever going to find a woman that I was the slightest bit interested in. When Charlie met Leona, he said that I had found myself a real knockout foxy lady. After Charlie walked away, Leona asked me what he had meant. I told her that he meant that she was exceptionally beautiful.

After I showed Leona around and explained how we refurbished antiques, we went down to the main street in New Hope. She saw the trains and said, "Paul, the trains haven't changed very much. Haven't any of your inventors tried to improve them?"

"The trains in New Hope are very old and they are only used to take tourists on a short ride. I'll have to take you for a ride on one of our new trains and stay in New York City for a long weekend—that will really impress you. New York City has some of the tallest buildings in the United States. We can go to the top of the Empire State Building and see the entire city from there."

She kissed me on the cheek and said, "I would love to travel with you, Paul. You make me happy when I am with you."

"The best day of my life is when I met you."

She held my hand as we walked through some of the shops. We walked across the bridge to Lambertville, New Jersey, and had an early dinner at one of my favorite restaurants.

Each day, I took her to different places that I thought might interest her such as the art museum and the Franklin Institute in Philadelphia. The IMAX Theater in the Franklin Institute seemed a little bit scary to her, and she kept closing her eyes, but Leona told me that she enjoyed the show.

On Friday, April 14, after a stroll through Washington Crossing State Park and a late lunch at a nearby inn, I said, "I'm running out of places to take you. Is there anywhere that you would like to go that might interest you?"

"I would like to go to your home and watch one of your videos."

It was late afternoon when we arrived home and I put on one of my favorite movies. She cuddled up next to me, pulled me close, and started kissing me. As I returned her kisses, I could feel the fire building in both of us. Finally she whispered, "Let's go to bed."

Leona took me by the hand and led me up to my bedroom. We fell asleep in each other's arms. When I awoke, I looked at the clock and saw that it was ten o'clock. Leona was gone so I called out to her, but there was no answer.

I got out of bed, put on my robe, and looked in the spare bedroom. Leona wasn't there and her uniform was missing—except for the apron on the bed. I knew at once what she had done! Somehow Leona had gotten through the mirror and was going to try to stop John Wilkes Booth from assassinating Lincoln.

I dressed as fast as I could, went through the mirror, and closed the hotel room door behind me. I raced down the steps and onto the street in front of the National Hotel, and headed for Ford's Theater. When I ran around the corner, I saw a large crowd gathering outside of the theater. It was 10:25 p.m. when I was close enough to hear someone say that the president had been shot.

A man standing by the door shouted, "Get that colored woman—she was trying to get in to see the president. She is probably an accomplice!"

I saw Leona making her way through the crowd, but no one saw her in the confusion. I grabbed her by the arm and said, "Don't say anything!" I pulled the shawl that she was wearing up over her head so that just part of her face was showing and said, "Keep your head down and your hands under the shawl." I put my arm around her and said, "I'll guide you. Don't make a sound."

As we were walking out of the crowded area, a man asked, "Did you see the colored woman that he wants us to stop?"

"No, I did not. I'm just trying to get my wife out of this crowd. She's feeling quite ill with all that has happened. We were in the theater when a man shot the president and jumped onto the stage, shouted something, and ran away limping."

"That must be a horrible experience for her to have witnessed," he said. Then he shouted to the crowd, "Make way—this lady is very sick. Let her get some air. She just witnessed the president being shot."

Instead of moving out of the way, people started blocking our way and pushing in front of us. They were shouting out questions at us. One man shouted, "Is he wounded or dead?" Another woman shouted, "Did you see who shot the president?" I was struggling to keep Leona covered with the shawl while pushing my way out of the crowd. I answered, "I don't know how badly the president has been injured—and we didn't get a good look at the man that shot him. All I know is that he jumped onto the stage and escaped."

I was getting worried that I wouldn't get Leona out of the crowd without someone pulling the shawl from her head and discovering who she was. I held the shawl over her head and pushed and shoved until we finally broke out of the mob.

We walked slowly until we got around the corner and then we picked up the pace. I told her not to look up until I got her back to safety. She was crying and saying that they wouldn't listen to her. I tried to calm her down as we walked back to the hotel.

When we were safely inside the hotel, I pulled the shawl off of her head. We made our way through the mirror back to the safety of my foyer. I pulled her close and said, "You scared me! I thought that I had lost you forever. So many things could have happened. You could have been hanged as an accomplice! Why did you do it and how did you get through the mirror without me?"

Leona tearfully replied, "I tried to get through the mirror and it wouldn't work for me. I found a pair of your gloves in a coat pocket in the closet. I put them on and when I put my hand on the glass it started to shimmer, and I was able to walk through the mirror as easily as you do.

"I was just trying to save President Lincoln, but no one would listen to me when I told them that the president was in danger. They refused to let me in the theater, but a man standing by the entrance sent me to the bar next door. He told me that I would find Mr. John Parker there. He was the president's bodyguard.

"When I found Mr. Parker, he was drunk. I told him that President Lincoln was in danger. He laughed at me and shouted that I was crazy. He told me not to bother him again or he would arrest me and throw me in jail. Mr. Parker is the man that was shouting that I was an accomplice."

"I can't blame you for trying to save President Lincoln. If I were you, I may have done the same thing, but it's history now and you are part of the future. Let's go back to bed and we'll talk about our future tomorrow."

I held her in my arms until she fell asleep. The next morning, she kissed me on the cheek and said, "I love you, Paul."

"I love you too, Leona. Would you like to be my wife one day and live with me for the rest of our lives?"

"Yes. I think we could make a good life together, but the first thing we have to do is get rid of that mirror."

"I agree. Let's go downstairs and cover it up. Charlie and I can remove it on Monday morning. I'm sure that you and I can find something else to place on that wall."

I took an old blanket out of the linen closet, and we started covering the mirror with it. When I touched the center of the glass with the blanket, a strange thing happened. The glass felt solid!

Leona looked at me and asked, "What is wrong?"

I pulled back the blanket and put my hand on the center of the mirror and answered, "The glass is solid. My hand won't go through it. I think the portal to the past has closed!"

"Well, I was going to stay with you anyway. Do you think that somehow the mirror knew?"

"Maybe there was a reason for the portal to open. I don't think that it had anything to do with you trying to save President Lincoln's life. I think that I was sent back in time to save you from being murdered by John Wilkes Booth or one of his men."

"That is the story that I want to believe. I think that the mirror wanted you to be my knight in shining armor—the man that I have dreamed about since I was a little girl."

After a long embrace, we continued to cover the mirror. On Monday morning, Charlie and I took the mirror back to my shop, packed it in a large wooden case, and sealed it. On the outside of the case, I painted in large black letters, "Do Not Open," and then we stored it in the back of the warehouse.

Charlie asked why I was taking the mirror down and storing it. I told him that Leona and I thought that something else might look better in the foyer. He said, "Just leave it to a woman. You bring them into your home and they want to change everything around."

"Well, women have a special touch. They can decorate a house better than a man can. I'm not going to sell the mirror because Leona may want to redecorate the house again one day and have a need for it."

Three months later, Leona and I were married. We spent our honeymoon in Hawaii. Flying in the airplane was a new experience for Leona. After all, she was just getting used to driving in traffic. Teaching her how to drive was a hair-raising experience.

Now, after three years of marriage, she's a pro at almost everything.

Leona gives Kathy Wilson a break in my office since she learned how to type—and she has just about mastered the computer.

We never talk about the mirror. I guess we choose to try to forget about it and put it in the past where it belongs. After all, it is part of history.

***

THE NEVER-ENDING ROAD

Hello, I am the Keeper of the Never-Ending Road. My name is not important. Over many years—more than I have bothered to count—I have answered to many names. All of them have been good, I assure you. At present, I am content if the people that I meet just call me Keeper.

My job is maintaining the Never-Ending Road and its unending variety of fantastic vacation destinations. You may say that you have never heard of my road or me—and that is probably true because, if you want to find my road, you have to receive a written invitation in the mail. It comes with detailed instructions that must be followed to the letter. I only send my invitations to a select few. In fact, I have a young man arriving here this morning that has just finished his vacation. Let me tell you his story.

Two months ago on a sunny June morning a young man in Holland, Pennsylvania, walked out of his townhouse. He was walking down to his curbside mailbox just as the mailman was pulling up in his little jeep delivery truck.

"Good morning, Robert," the mailman said.

"Good morning, Charlie. Except for bills, do you have anything good in today's delivery for me?"

"This letter looks like some kind of an invitation." Charlie handed an envelope to Robert. It had a gold border and was addressed to Mr. Robert Wright.

"Thank you, Charlie, and have a nice day."

Robert walked up to his office and opened the mail. He opened the bills first and then he picked up the envelope with the gold border. It looked interesting and he was curious and decided to read it before throwing it away with the rest of the junk mail.

Robert read the invitation.

The Keeper of the Never-Ending Road
P.O. Box 101
New Albany, PA, 18854

Mr. Robert Wright:

You are cordially invited to drive on the Never-Ending Road. I know that you are a high school history teacher and enjoy teaching and studying world history. For this reason, you qualify for a two-week, all-expense paid vacation on the Never-Ending Road.

By driving on my Never-Ending Road, you can travel to any place in the world—at any point in time in the past—that you wish. I guarantee that you will have a safe trip. Safety features have been built into the Never-Ending Road so that you can be extracted from any time period immediately if you are in the slightest bit of danger.

This is not a hoax! This is a real vacation! If you are interested, please sign the enclosed form and return it in the postage-paid envelope. If you are not interested, please destroy this invitation by burning or shredding it. Do not pass this invitation on to anyone else, since it is meant only for you!

Sincerely Yours,
The Keeper of the Never-Ending Road

Robert put the invitation down on the desk and said, "This guy is nuts." He was ready to tear the invitation to shreds and throw it in the wastebasket when he had second thoughts. Why would this man send out an invitation knowing that anyone reading it would chuck it in the trash? I have heard of people trying to invent time machines. There have been lots of science fiction books written on time travel and many scientists think that it may be possible to travel through time and space to other dimensions. Maybe he is some kind of an inventor that has discovered how to travel through time. How does he know my occupation and where I live? It could be some of the kids in my classroom pulling a hoax on me, but this is too elaborate. How could they get a post office box in New Albany?

Robert's curiosity was so strong that he signed the form and put it in the postage-paid return envelope. Later that evening, he put it in his mailbox for Charlie. He thought that the only thing that could happen would be that he wouldn't get an answer.

A week later, Robert looked in his mailbox and found a large envelope addressed to him from New Albany. He took it up to his office, sat down at his desk, and opened it. It contained a letter and maps.

Robert read the letter.

> The Keeper of the Never-Ending Road
> P. O. Box 101
> New Albany, PA, 18854
>
> Mr. Robert Wright:
>
> Thank you for accepting my invitation for your all-expense paid two-week vacation on my Never-Ending Road. Your vacation will begin on Monday, August 7, at 10:00 a.m., and end on Sunday, August 20, at 5:00 p.m. Please arrive promptly as I have other appointments after yours, and would like to be finished with all of my appointments at 1:00 p.m. Your orientation will take approximately one half hour.

You will find maps and explicit instructions in this envelope that will tell you how to get to my home at the entrance to the Never-Ending Road. Please study them and be familiar with them so that you will not get lost.

I have enclosed a list of hotels and motels in the area. I strongly recommend that you consider staying at one of them on Sunday evening, so that you will not be fatigued from driving during the early morning hours. I suggest that you have breakfast before arriving at my home since it is not included on the first morning of your vacation.

Sincerely Yours
The Keeper of the Never-Ending Road

Robert thought again that this could be a joke thought up by one of his friends or students just to get him to drive upstate on a fool's errand. Still curious, he decided to find out whether this Never-Ending Road was real or a well-organized joke. If it was a joke, he was hoping that the kids in his class didn't find out or he would never live it down.

Robert made reservations at one of the motels in Clarks Summit for the evening of Sunday, August 6. The motel was not far from his destination on Route 87.

On Sunday, August 6, Robert put his suitcase in his trunk and began the long ride up to Clarks Summit. When he reached the exit, he drove about a mile up Route 6 to the motel. That evening, he had trouble sleeping and kept wondering whether or not he was on a wild goose chase—and whether there really was a Keeper of a Never-Ending Road.

On Monday, Robert showered and had breakfast at the motel. After he checked out, he drove up Route 6 and then turned left on Route 87. Then he read the instructions to his final destination. "After turning onto Route 87, look for a heavily wooded area on the left. You will see a small brown wooden sign with a yellow arrow painted on it.

The sign is near the left shoulder of the road. When you reach the end of the point of the arrow painted on the sign, make an immediate left turn onto the driveway. The driveway will lead you to my home."

Robert drove along Route 87 until he spotted the sign. He stopped the car in front of the sign and looked across the road. There was no driveway at the end of the arrow. There was nothing but bushes and trees. *That's it! I've been had! I wonder who thought up this scheme. I guess I'll find out when I get back home.*

Furious at his stupidity in believing that a Never-Ending Road even existed, he started to turn the car around. He pulled up next to the sign on the left shoulder of the road at the end of the point of the arrow and was ready to put the car in reverse. Suddenly, the brush in front of him parted, revealing a gravel driveway between the trees. *I have to be seeing things! Where did that driveway come from and what made that brush move? This is really scary and it's freaking me out. Maybe I should turn around and go back home.*

Robert sat there with his foot on the brake pedal for a few seconds while his curiosity was building. He had to see what was on the other end of the driveway, so he took his foot of the brake. As he moved slowly along the driveway, he looked in the rearview mirror and noticed that the brush was moving back in place, covering the driveway behind him. It was impossible for him to back out!

How am I going to get out of here? He started to drive a little faster, trying not to hit a tree. The faster he drove, the quicker the brush covered the driveway behind him.

Finally, Robert drove into a clearing and was amazed to see a large stone house in the middle of the open area. He was hoping that—if this was not the home of the Keeper of the Never-Ending Road—the owner could tell him how to get back on the highway. As he pulled up near the house, he looked at his watch. It was exactly ten o'clock.

Robert got out of the car and, as he was walking up the steps, the front door opened. A tall elderly gentleman with gray hair in a black tuxedo was standing in front of him. "Good morning," he said.

"Good morning," Robert replied.

"Welcome to my home, Mr. Wright."

Robert nodded.

The man stepped aside and allowed Robert to pass through the front door. "Please come in, Mr. Wright. I'm glad to see that you are punctual, Mr. Wright."

Robert felt uncomfortable with all the formality.

"May I call you Robert?"

"Yes, you may."

"And what can I call you?"

"The Keeper of the Never-Ending Road."

"That's rather long, don't you think. And it's more of a title than a name."

The Keeper shrugged. "Some names are titles, but you may call me Keeper. Just consider it a first name. It's the best I can do to keep our conversation as informal as possible. Come into my living room, sit down, and relax. I'll start your orientation as soon as you are comfortable."

Robert tried not to think of the guy as crazy. He preferred eccentric, especially after watching the driveway disappear.

Robert sat on the sofa in front of the tea table while the Keeper poured hot tea into two china teacups from a china teapot. Robert took a lump of sugar from the bowl on the table and put it into his cup, stirring it a little with his spoon. As he was taking a sip, his hand was shaking a little from his experience on the driveway.

The Keeper could see that Robert was nervous and said, "I know that you are wondering how you can get back on the highway if you choose to leave. If you follow the driveway, you will see a black sign with white lettering that says 'Exit.' There is also a white arrow pointing in the direction that you must drive. The brush will part and you can drive down the gravel road onto the highway—just as easily as you drove up to my home."

"The disappearing driveway really shook me up."

"The driveways are harmless and I only use them to conceal my property. There are more and, if you decide to go home, the one on my exit driveway is the only one that you will have to use. But I know that you are curious about my Never-Ending Road or you would not be here, so let me tell you all about it. The road is actually a highway through time! It is a single-lane paved highway. There is plenty of room to pass other travelers if you find their vehicles parked near the side of the road. You can stop anywhere that you wish and visit any country, including the United States, and any time period that you are interested in. Each state, country, and time period that you can travel to is clearly marked on signs along the road. Please be courteous when you park—and leave enough room for other travelers to pass."

"Do I get out of my car and walk into these places?"

"No. There are transporter rooms along the edge of the road at each state or country for different periods in time. They are painted light blue and are seven feet tall and four feet square. All that you have to do is open the door, walk inside, and close and lock the door. You must change into the clothing that was placed inside of the transporter and take the purse, wallet, or bag of money with you to use on your visit.

"When you are ready to enter the time zone, the only thing that you must do is move the lever on the wall panel of the transporter room to the enter position. If you want to return to the Never-Ending Road, the lever must be moved to the return position."

"If I travel back in time in a foreign country, how will I be able to speak to the people?"

"Do not to worry about speaking the language in any country that you chose to visit. You will understand the citizens—and they will understand you. The transporter will automatically change your language and you will understand the language in the country that you are visiting. You will not even realize that you are conversing in another language. When you return to the Never-Ending Road, you will speak in your own language again.

"I warn you, do not to take anything with you from the present, and do not bring anything or anyone with you when you return, because it could have a serious impact on the present. Please change back into your own clothing in the transporter room before leaving it. Everything else is to be left in the transporter. Do you have any more questions?"

"It is very hard for me to believe all that you have told me. What would happen if I decide not to travel on the Never-Ending Road?"

"Nothing will happen except that you will lose the best vacation opportunity that you have ever had. All that you have to do is get into your car, drive to the exit sign, and go home. But I know that you are extremely curious or you would not be here. Here is the control unit that opens the transporters." He handed Robert a small unit that looked like an electronic keypad for a car door key hanging on a silver neck chain. "Hang this around your neck. When you are not wearing it, keep it in a safe place. Do not give it to anyone to hold for you—and do not let anyone see it. It is waterproof and heat resistant.

"To open the transporter door, just push the unlock button on the control unit and the door will open. When you are safely inside push the lock button and the door will close. Once you leave the transporter in the place that you are visiting, push the lock button, the door will close, and the transporter will become invisible. When you wish to return to the Never-Ending Road, just push the unlock button and the transporter will reappear with the door open in front of you, no matter where you are."

"If I don't like the place that I have picked, can I leave and go to another destination?"

"Yes, just drive to another destination that might interest you. If you want to leave your vacation early or when your two weeks are over and it is time to go home and you are back on The Never-Ending Road, just get into your car. Push the red button on the control unit and start driving. The Never-Ending Road will bring you back to my home in a matter of minutes where you must drop off the control unit. If for some reason I do not answer the door when you ring the bell, just drop the control unit in the wooden basket next to the front door.

"How do I find the entrance to the Never-Ending Road?"

"The entrance to The Never-Ending Road is just down the driveway. Make the first right turn at the brown sign with the yellow arrow. If you change your mind at the last minute and wish to go home, don't make the turn. Just go straight down the driveway to the exit sign. You will see a wooden basket under the exit sign. All you need to do is drop the control unit into it, and follow the exit road to the main highway."

The Keeper stood up and held out his right hand. Robert stood up and shook hands with the Keeper and then the Keeper said, "Good luck." Then he escorted Robert to the front door.

As Robert was walking out of the front door, the Keeper said, "There is one thing that I forgot to mention. When you arrive at a destination, if someone recognizes you and calls you by another name, answer to that name and agree with that person on anything that they say or ask you to do. Give them answers and do not tell them who you really are." The Keeper then closed the door behind Robert before he could ask any questions.

I wonder why the Keeper said that. I guess it's important and I'll have to figure out what he meant if and when I arrive at a destination.

Robert got in his car and started the engine. He proceeded to drive along the gravel driveway.

Hesitating, he stopped the car at the brown sign with the yellow arrow marking the entrance to the Never-Ending Road. In the distance, he could see the exit sign. Robert wondered what he should do. His curiosity was at the point that he could make no other decision. He put the transporter control unit and chain around his neck, and his foot went from the brake to the accelerator as he made a sharp right turn onto the Never-Ending Road.

Robert drove to a wooded area where it looked as if it came to a dead end. But as he approached, the brush parted again to reveal more of the road. He drove for about a quarter of a mile and, when he pulled out of the woods, he found himself on a paved single-lane highway leading into a vast open area. The road was clearly visible for miles ahead, but the area on each side of the road seemed to be covered in some sort of light fog. There were transporter rooms on each side of the road and signs marking each place—and time periods for the transporters.

A car was parked on the right side of the road near a sign that read, "Philadelphia, 1776." Seeing no occupant, he pulled over and parked in front of it. Robert got out of the car and saw that one of the transporters was missing. He walked over to the edge of the road and tried to see through the mist. He was amazed at what he saw. He could see the outline of Independence Hall in the distance. Closer, he could make out people dressed in Colonial fashion, and there were horse-drawn carriages passing by.

This has to be real! I'm looking at Colonial Philadelphia! The person that owns the car that's parked behind me must be having a great vacation. I'm not going to pick the first place that I see. Let me look around.

Walking to the other side of the road, Robert looked into Gettysburg, 1863. It seemed pretty quiet, but since he didn't know the exact date and it appeared to be summer, he wasn't about to take a chance and have a vacation in the middle of a battle zone. Robert got back into the car and continued to drive on the Never-Ending Road.

Robert drove slowly past the signs for Palos, Spain 1492, Paris, France 1789, and Vienna, Austria, 1791. He finally stopped at Pompeii, Italy, AD 79. He parked, got out, and peered through the mist. He could make out people, horses, and chariots. Everyone seemed to be going about his or her business, and it looked quite peaceful. He knew that Mount Vesuvius erupted in AD 79 and covered Pompeii with volcanic ash, but he was curious to see what it was like before the city was destroyed.

Robert had been to the ruins of Pompeii several times on trips to Italy—and he was completely fascinated with the ancient city. He made up his mind that this was the place where he was going to spend his vacation. He walked over to a transporter and pushed the unlock button on his control unit—instantly the door slid open on a hydraulic track.

After walking inside the transporter, Robert pushed the lock button on his control unit and the hydraulic door closed. On a hook on the wall of the transporter was a white toga that Robert had to wear. A pair of leather sandals was on the floor below the toga. After he had changed and hung his clothes on the hook, he thought, *I must look as if I am dressed to go to a college toga party.*

A thick cloth bag with long leather drawstrings contained extra clothing. A small cloth bag with long leather drawstrings was next to the clothing bag. When Robert picked it up, it felt very heavy. When he opened it, he knew why. The bag was full of ancient Roman coins for him to spend on his vacation in Pompeii.

Robert tied the moneybag around his waist, walked over to

the control panel, and pushed the lever to the enter position. The transporter hummed faintly and seemed to lift slightly off of the ground. Within only a few seconds, the humming stopped and the transporter seemed to settle back on the ground. A green light on the panel started to flash. The printing under it read, "It is safe to exit when this light is flashing."

Excited at what he was about to see, Robert quickly pushed the unlock button on the control unit. The hydraulic door opened to a sight that he could have never imagined in his wildest dreams. He was on a hill looking down at the ancient city of Pompeii!

He stepped out of the transporter and pushed the lock button on the control unit without looking back at it. When he turned around to see what was behind him, he saw only a wooded area about a hundred feet away. The transporter had vanished! He remembered that the Keeper had told him that the transporter would disappear when he pushed the lock button on the control unit, but he was nervous. He wanted to see if the transporter would reappear wherever he was, so he walked up to the wooded area and pushed the unlock button on the control unit. The transporter instantly appeared in front of him and the hydraulic door was open!

Relieved, Robert reached in and took out the bag of extra clothing that he had forgotten in his excitement, and then he pushed the lock button on the control unit. The transporter door closed and it instantly vanished again. He put the bag of clothing over his shoulder like a sailor, and walked toward Pompeii.

As he walked through the city, he was amazed at the pristine buildings and their architecture. He had walked through the ruins of the ancient city several times, but there was no comparison to the undamaged city that he was looking at. It looked so much better than the computer-generated buildings that he had seen. The citizens of Pompeii impressed him as they went about their everyday business. They were alive and well with no knowledge of the disaster that was about to happen. The Roman soldiers were the real thing as they walked along the streets and rode on their horse-drawn chariots. It was hard for him to imagine that he was walking through Pompeii and it was alive and well.

Robert decided to walk to the Forum, which was the busiest

shopping area of ancient Pompeii. As he was walking through the Forum looking at the wares and produce being sold at various shops and stands, a man came running in his direction, shouting, "Marcus! Marcus Valerius!" Robert just stood there not knowing what to say. When the man got close to Robert, he exclaimed, "You look just like your father, Senator Marcellus Valerius! How are your mother, Aurelia, and your father? Are they in good health?

Robert was ready to tell the man that he was mistaken when he remembered what the Keeper had told him as he was leaving. He thought that maybe this was set up for some reason by the Keeper. Robert knew that he had to say something to the man, so he answered, "My father and mother are just fine. They are not with me. I am traveling alone."

"What are you doing here in Pompeii, Marcus?"

"I wanted to see what it was like here in Pompeii. I'm sorry, but I can't remember you. Do I know you?"

"I'm Antonius Gallus, a friend of your family. I have to admit that I haven't seen them in several years. You were just a boy, but it is truly amazing how much you resemble your father! Where are you staying?"

"I haven't found any lodging yet. I only just arrived and haven't really looked for a place to stay."

"There is no need to look. You shall stay with my wife and me while you are here in Pompeii. You will be our guest! Your father has helped me in the past and I wish to return the favor."

"Thank you, but I wouldn't want to cause you any inconvenience. I can find a place to stay."

"Don't worry you won't cause me any inconvenience. I have a very large home with plenty of room for guests. My children are all grown and moved away after they were married. The house is almost empty except for my wife and the servants, and my niece who just came to visit with us this morning. My wife and I love to have people over as guests. It seems to bring our home back to life. Come—walk with me to my home!"

Robert thanked his newfound friend for his hospitality and followed him to his home. As they walked and talked, Antonius kept referring to Robert as Marcus. Robert knew that Antonius recognized him as Marcus Valerius and it might be that the Keeper wanted him to assume that identity. While he was in Pompeii, he decided that it would be best if he answered to Marcus Valerius.

When they arrived at the house, Antonius ushered Robert through the front door. Once they reached the main great room, which had a skylight and a reflecting pool in the center, Antonius stopped and said, “Welcome to my home, Marcus.” Then Antonius called out, “Everyone come and meet, Marcus Valerius the son of my friend, Senator Marcellus Valerius.”

Instantly, a man and two women came out and Antonius introduced Robert to them. The man was Servius and the women were Varinia and Flavia. They were his servants. If Robert needed anything at any time, they would be at his service.

Robert set his bag of clean clothing on the floor. Antonius told the servants to take the bag to one of the guest rooms and make it ready for Marcus. Servius picked up the bag and walked toward the guest room with Varinia and Flavia. Two women came out of the garden and approached Antonius and Robert.

The middle-aged woman was very attractive with long brown hair pulled up on top and in back of her head. Antonius introduced her to Robert as his wife, Livia. Then Antonius introduced his niece, Fabia Sidonius. The young woman had only just arrived that morning to visit. Fabia had blue eyes and long blonde hair that was pulled back in the same style as her aunt.

Antonius said, “Come let us all go out into the garden where we can sit and talk for a while until dinner is ready.” As they were walking out to the garden, he looked at Robert and said, “Tomorrow maybe you and Fabia would like to explore our fair city together.”

Robert looked at Fabia and said, “I would like that, if she would like me to accompany her.”

Fabia replied, “I think that I would enjoy exploring Pompeii with you, Marcus.”

“Very good,” said Antonius. “I enjoy seeing young people do things together.”

Everyone sat on stone benches and light green cushions around a small fountain in the garden. The garden contained many flowers and herbs, including pink and yellow Snapdragons, bluebells, green dill herbs, and silver thyme. The garden was surrounded by stone walls, giving it the appearance of an oasis within the bustling city.

Antonius asked Fabia and Robert what they would most like to see in Pompeii. Fabia said that she would like to see everything, while Robert told him that he also wanted to see everything, but he really wanted to see the Temple of Venus first. Antonius told them that it would take a few days to see everything, but they had plenty of time. He told Robert that the Temple of Venus had been destroyed in an earthquake several years earlier, and all that he could see would be the ruins. He said the Temple of Apollo was quite interesting, and that he might like to see it instead of a ruined temple.

While they were waiting for dinner to be served, Antonius and Livia spoke of their farms several days' journey south of Pompeii.

Fabia asked, "Do you have many slaves working your lands?"

Livia answered, "We have no slaves. All of our servants and farm laborers are free, and we pay them salaries. Antonius and I don't believe in slavery. We gave all of our servants their freedom as soon as we bought them and gave them a choice of being paid to work for us or leaving. Most of them decided to stay while others went back to their homelands to find their families that they had been forcefully taken away from."

Fabia replied, "You and Antonius are truly wonderful people. I wish there were more citizens in this country like you."

"There are other people in this country that free their slaves, but we are a minority," said Livia.

A few moments later, everyone went into the dining room for dinner. After dinner, Antonius showed Robert and Fabia where the baths were located down the hallway—one for men and one for women. Then he showed them to their bedrooms and wished them both a good night.

After a warm bath, Robert climbed up the steps and out of the bath. He looked for his clothes, but they were gone. In their place, he found some large towels. He dried off, wrapped himself in the towels, and walked out of the room. On the way to his bedroom, he met Fabia who was also wrapped in towels. He said, "I see that you have also lost your clothing."

Blushing, she replied, "Yes, I did. I guess that Varinia put them in my room. I saw her pick them up and leave the towels for me."

"I didn't see anyone. I guess that I had my back turned when Servius made the exchange. Well, goodnight again, and I will see you in the morning."

Fabia said goodnight and they went to their bedrooms.

During breakfast, Antonius told Robert and Fabia the places that they should visit first. Livia said that she thought that Marcus and Fabia looked as if they would make a wonderful couple, which made Fabia blush. Robert just smiled.

After they left the house and were walking toward the Forum, Robert said, "Fabia, did you get the impression that Antonius and Livia are matchmakers—and they would like us to be a lot more than just casual friends?"

"Yes, I did." She smiled at Robert. "You never know what will happen, but having a male companion when walking through a strange city is nice." She took him by the hand. "Come with me. You wanted to see the Temple of Venus. Even though it was destroyed in the earthquake, the ruins may interest you. I passed it when I arrived yesterday and I know where it is."

As they walked through the crowded Forum to the Temple of Venus, Robert thought, *I'm attracted to Fabia, but I can't allow myself to fall in love with her. What if she was to fall in love with me I can't take her back home with me, and I don't think that I can stay here in ancient Italy. I have to try to keep this a casual friendship.*

They walked through the ruins of the Temple of Venus and explored some of the city. They went back to the Forum and checked out some of the wares that the merchants were selling. Their next stop was on a side street at a Tavola Calda, which reminded Robert of a fast food restaurant. Each of them had a goblet of wine and a bowl of soup for lunch.

After lunch, they visited the Temple of Apollo and then they walked down to the seaport. At the docks, they saw merchant ships being unloaded and reloaded. They also walked to a secluded spot on the beach away from the busy docks.

On the beach, they talked mainly about things that they had seen during their walk. As they were talking and laughing, Robert kept thinking that he would love to hold this beautiful woman in his arms and kiss her sweet lips. It was hard for him to control his emotions, but he knew that he must be strong. He could not allow himself to weaken.

They went home and had dinner with Antonius and Livia. Livia asked them if they had enjoyed their walk and if they had found it interesting. Fabia said that it was very interesting, especially since she had a handsome man as a chaperone. Robert smiled at her compliment and said that he had a very beautiful woman holding onto his hand, and that he couldn't wait until the next day to see more of the city with her.

After breakfast, Robert and Fabia visited another section of the city. After lunch at another Tavola Calda, they ended up sitting on the beach again. Robert couldn't stop himself from gazing into her beautiful blue eyes. The urge to kiss her that was welling up inside of him became overpowering. He couldn't resist it any longer! He kissed her on the lips, thinking that he was going to get a very hard slap on the face. To his surprise, she pulled him close and they were soon locked in a passionate embrace. When they separated, Fabia said, "I was wondering when you were going to kiss me."

Robert—thinking of something to say and knowing that he couldn't tell her the truth—replied, "I shouldn't have done that. It's too soon in our relationship. Please forgive me."

Fabia stroked his face with her hand and said, "There is nothing to forgive. I feel the same way and I am just as much responsible as you are." Then she pulled Robert close and they kissed again.

When they left the beach, they walked back to the house. As they got near the front door, they saw servants carrying jugs of water into the house. Inside, they saw Antonius telling the servants where to put the jugs. Robert asked Antonius why they needed water since the house had its own well. Antonius told him that most of the wells in Pompeii—including his own—had suddenly gone dry. They had been getting water from one of the main wells in the city.

Robert instantly knew what was happening from his knowledge of the history of Pompeii. Ten days before the eruption of Mount Vesuvius, the wells in Pompeii suddenly went dry.

How could he tell Antonius of the impending danger without

changing something in history? How could he tell Fabia? He didn't want them to suffer the fate that so many of Pompeii's citizens were about to experience.

Robert had an idea! "Antonius, this looks like a serious situation. You may want to consider moving to your farms in the south for a while. Maybe the water will eventually return to the wells."

"That is a good suggestion, my young friend," said Antonius. "You are just as sharp as your father in your thinking, but I prefer to wait a little longer. Maybe our water will return to our wells in a few days."

"If the water doesn't return in a few days and the main wells start to dry up, it will cause a serious water shortage, and be very hard for the citizens in Pompeii to survive. If that happens, I hope you will consider leaving the city as soon as possible."

"You are a very good man to be so concerned about our welfare and I am glad to have met you. I promise you that if the main wells start to dry up, Livia and I will leave Pompeii—and I would like you and Fabia to come with us."

Robert thanked Antonius for his kind invitation. He knew that he was only allowed to stay for two weeks and that his vacation had to end. He had to say something so he told Antonius that his family was expecting him to return home soon.

Fabia said, "I would love to go with you and Livia, but I have the same problem as Marcus. I promised to return home to my parents after my stay here in Pompeii."

Antonius said, "We would love to have the two of you spend more time with us, but I can understand that your parents miss you and want you to return home. Well, we will make the best of it and enjoy the rest of your stay—until it is time for all of us to go our separate ways."

The next morning after breakfast with Antonius and Livia, Robert and Fabia went out to explore. As they walked through the Forum, they heard a man yelling, "Stop that thief!" The man had a large stick in his hand and was chasing a little boy. The boy was running as fast as he could while carrying a melon in his arms.

Two nearby soldiers got into the chase after the boy. The boy tripped, hitting his knees hard on the paving stones, and the melon flew out of his arms. It broke into several pieces when it landed. The boy was crying in pain when the man grabbed him by the arm. He was ready to hit him with the stick when Robert ran up and grabbed his arm, pulling him back and almost knocking him off balance.

Robert shouted, "Leave the child alone! Can't you see that he is injured?"

"He stole that melon from my stand. He deserves to be punished! Just look at my melon! I can't even sell it!"

The soldiers caught up and one said to Robert, "Who are you to stop this man from dealing out punishment to this little thief?"

Fabia, who now was standing next to Robert, said calmly, "This is Marcus Valerius the son of Senator Marcellus Valerius."

As soon as the soldier heard the name, he said, "I'm sorry, sir. I didn't know who you were. I was only doing my duty."

"I understand," said Robert. Then he handed the merchant some coins and said, "This should be enough to pay for your melon."

The merchant took the money and said, "Thank you, sir. You are most generous. I'm sorry that I didn't recognize you." Then he walked away.

Robert handed the soldiers each some coins and told them that it was for a job well done. He and Fabia would take care of the child. The soldiers thanked him and went on their way.

After the soldiers left, Fabia tried to calm the frightened boy. Wiping his tears, she asked where his mother and father were. He said that his mother was dead and he didn't have a father. As she stroked his dark blond hair, she asked his name and why he had taken the melon. He told her that his name was Silvanus. His little sister, Junia, was hungry and they had not eaten in two days. Fabia asked if he was hungry and he told her that he was much stronger than his six-year-old sister. He was nine years old—and he could do without food longer than his sister could.

Fabia asked Silvanus to take them to his sister. Robert wanted to carry him because his little knees were skinned and bloody, but Silvanus wanted to walk. He said that he was strong and the pain didn't bother him. Silvanus led them around the corner to an abandoned building. They went inside and he led them to a little girl with light blonde hair and blue eyes. She was on the floor in a corner and was surprised when she looked up at them.

Silvanus said, “Don’t be afraid, Junia. They are nice people. They won’t hurt you.”

Fabia said, “The poor child is weak, Marcus. We must get them out of here.”

Robert picked up Junia and cradled her in his arms. Speaking softly and calmly, he said, “Don’t be afraid. We won’t hurt you. We are going to take you to a nice place where you can have something to eat and sleep in a nice warm bed.” He turned to Fabia and said, “Let’s take them back to the house. I don’t think Antonius and Livia will mind.”

When they returned to the house, they found Antonius on the bench near the empty fountain. Livia was on her knees transplanting some flowers.

Antonius got up off the bench when he saw the children and asked, “What do we have here?”

Fabia replied, “Two orphan children that we found living on the streets and about to starve to death.”

Livia came over to see the children and said, “The poor little children are in dreadful shape. We must feed them and get them cleaned up. Bring them into the house!”

Everyone went into the great room and Robert put Junia on a bench. Silvanus sat down beside her. Livia called to the servants and had Flavia prepare food for the children. She told Servius to get clean water and sent Varinia for some clean cloth and ointment for Silvanus’s knees.

When everything was brought out, Fabia said, “Let me handle this. I have experience cleaning and dressing wounds.” Fabia cleaned Silvanus’s knees and put the ointment on them. It seemed almost as if she had been trained in modern nursing. She said, “I’ll put more ointment on his knees and bandage them after the children are bathed.”

Flavia entered the room and said that food was waiting for the children in the dining room. Everyone went into the dining room with the children. When they were seated at the table, Fabia said that since they hadn’t eaten in several days, they should eat slowly and not overeat or they would become sick. Since Junia was too weak to pick up her food, Livia picked it up and fed her by hand.

After the children ate, Fabia and Livia bathed Junia while Robert and Antonius took Silvanus into the bath and helped him clean up. Since Livia had some clothing left behind from her grandchildren's visits, they dressed the children and threw away their torn rags. Fabia put more ointment on the boy's knees and bandaged them. Livia had a small bedroom in the house that she used for her grandchildren when they came to visit. Fabia and Livia decided that it would be best if they put the children to bed so that they could get some rest.

At dinner, Robert and Fabia decided that they would go shopping and buy some new clothing for Silvanus and Junia in the morning. They were trying to decide what to do with the children since they were going their separate ways and couldn't take the children with them. Antonius said that he and Livia had some friends in the city that took in orphans to live with them. He and Livia would take the children to visit with their friends as soon as they had regained their strength.

Robert was worried about the children staying in Pompeii because he knew of the city's peril. *I hope that we didn't save the children from starvation only to be buried under the ash from Mount Vesuvius.* He knew that he couldn't tell anyone what was about to happen; he could only hope that the children would escape the volcano's wrath.

The next morning, Livia remarked how Junia seemed to be getting stronger because she was able to walk by holding onto her hand—and she was finally able to feed herself. She also said that the children looked very pale when they came to the house, but the color seemed to be returning to their faces.

After breakfast, Fabia kissed the children good-bye and said, "Marcus and I are going shopping to buy you some new clothing. Antonius and Livia are going to take care of you until we return."

Robert and Fabia picked up some beautiful new clothing and sandals for the children at the Forum. Fabia suggested that they buy some toys. When they returned to the house, their arms were so loaded with all kinds of things for the children that they were struggling to get the front door open.

Servius, who was carrying water back to the house, saw them and put his water jug down near the front step. "Let me help you," he said. He opened the door, took some of the gifts, and helped Robert and Fabia put them in the children's room. "You are like a married couple buying things for their children. Everyone is in the garden—and I know that the children will be delighted to see all of the things that you have bought for them."

Fabia and Robert went out to the garden and found Antonius and Livia playing with the children. The children were next to Livia on a bench near the fountain. Silvanus, Junia, and Livia were laughing at Antonius making funny faces.

Fabia said, "We have a surprise for you, Silvanus and Junia."

"What is it?" the children replied almost in unison.

"Come with us," Fabia answered.

Everyone followed Robert and Fabia into the children's bedroom. Livia had to hold Junia by the hand since she was still a little weak. When the children saw all of the gifts on their beds, they shrieked with joy and went immediately for the toys. Robert thought that they weren't much different from modern children.

Finally, the children started looking at the new clothing. Then they both started to cry. "What is wrong?" asked Fabia.

"We never had new clothes, and we only had broken toys that someone threw away," Silvanus answered, holding back his sobs. "Everyone here has been so good to Junia and me—and we love all of you. We will miss you when you send us away."

"Where do you think that we are going to send you?" asked Livia.

"Last night I heard Antonius say that he was going to give us to some of your friends that take in orphans."

Livia pulled him close and said, "Marcus and Fabia are leaving soon and Antonius and I want to make sure that you and Junia never have to go back to living on the streets. We just want you and Junia to be taken care of by a loving family. Do you understand what I am trying to tell you?"

"Yes," answered Silvanus.

"That's a good boy," said Livia. "Now let us all go out in the garden and we will play with your new toys."

After playing with the children for a little while, Robert and Fabia asked if it would be all right if they went out for a walk. Antonius told them to go out and have fun because young people should be with each other. Antonius told them that Livia and he enjoyed being with the children. Fabia and Robert kissed the children good-bye and they were on their way to explore the city again.

After a short walk, Robert and Fabia ended up on the beach again. After a few passionate moments of kissing, Fabia pushed Robert away and said, "We shouldn't be doing this! We are going to be leaving in a few days and may never see each other again."

"I guess that you are right," he said.

"When you marry, do you want to have children?"

"Yes. I would like to marry a woman just like you and have two beautiful children just like Silvanus and Junia."

She pulled him close and kissed him again. Then she moved away and stood up. "Come, we must go."

As they walked back to the house, she said, "We can't go back to the beach anymore. We must only remain friends while we are here in Pompeii."

Robert knew that she was right because he knew that he couldn't take her back with him, but he asked, "Why?"

"I am betrothed to another man and we are to be married when I return home."

Robert's heart sunk, and he could feel the pain of his loss in the pit of his stomach, but he knew that it was for the best. Fabia belonged in ancient Italy, and it was impossible for him to take her to the twenty-first century. Even if he could take Fabia with him, he knew that doing so could change the future. She may be the future mother of a child that was connected to someone of importance that would never be born because of him. *Maybe it's possible for me to come back and stay here with Fabia in ancient Italy. My future is still ahead of me. The Keeper might be able to do something to send me back to Fabia. I'll ask him when I return.*

For the next few days, they all played with the children in the garden after breakfast. In the afternoon, Robert and Fabia would walk through the city. They still talked and held hands as they were walking, but when Robert turned toward the beach, Fabia would make sure that they turned in another direction.

One evening during dinner, Antonius said, "Livia and I have decided to leave Pompeii for our farms in the south tomorrow morning. Marcus, I am taking your advice. The main wells in the city are getting very low and soon there won't be enough water for drinking."

"What about the children?" asked Fabia.

Livia replied, "We have decided not to leave the children with our friends—we are going to take them with us. They are such a pleasure to have around us that we have decided to adopt them."

Antonius said, "In the short time that they have been here, we have grown to love them—and we would miss them if we gave them to someone else. We are going to have them educated and give them our family name of Gallus, so that no one will ever look down on them. When they are grown, they will be able to hold their heads up high and be respected among their peers."

Robert was relieved that the children were going to be moved away from Pompeii. He said, "You are truly the most caring and wonderful people that I have ever met—and I am very fortunate to have known you."

Fabia was almost in tears. She said, "Marcus could not have expressed the same way that I feel about both of you any better." She gave each of them a big hug and a kiss on the cheek.

Early the next morning, everyone helped to load three horse-drawn carts with Antonius and Livia's most valuable possessions. Servius sat on one cart and Flavia and Varinia sat on another cart. Antonius put Silvanus and Junia in the back of the cart that he and Livia were going to drive. Robert asked Antonius where he had gotten the horses and carts. Antonius said that he owned stables in Pompeii and rented the horses and carts to merchants. It was just another source of his income.

Livia told Robert and Fabia that they were welcome to stay in the house until they were ready to go back to their homes. Antonius handed Robert a key to the house and showed him a loose stone next to the doorpost. He told him to put the key behind it when they were leaving. Robert and Fabia kissed the children and said their good-byes to the servants, Antonius, and Livia. They waved their final good-byes and the carts slowly rolled away.

After the carts turned a corner and disappeared from sight, Robert turned to Fabia and said, "I will miss them."

"I feel exactly the same way. I will miss the children most of all."

"When will you be going home?"

"Tomorrow afternoon during the Feast of Vulcan, the god of subterranean fire.

I thought that I might stay and watch the celebration for a little while and then leave when I've seen enough."

Robert knew that Mount Vesuvius was going to erupt at noon on the day after the Feast of Vulcan. Concerned about Fabia's safety, he asked, "How will you be leaving the city?"

"I rented a chariot when I arrived by ship. The driver picked me up at the docks north of Mount Vesuvius. He lives only a short walk from here. He knows that I will be at his home tomorrow afternoon. I will pay him his final payment when I am safely aboard the ship. The ship will leave on the evening tide and take me back to my home in Rome. Where do you live, Marcus?"

"At my father's home in the north near the mountains." Changing the subject he asked, "Would you like to enjoy the time that we have left by exploring more of Pompeii?"

"I would like that very much."

They walked through the winding city streets and ate at a Tavola Calda when they were hungry. In the Forum, they bought some bread and cheese for breakfast the next morning. When they were tired of walking, they went back to the house.

They talked and laughed until it started to get dark. Finally, Robert couldn't resist the urge any longer and he pulled Fabia close and kissed her on the cheek. To his surprise, Fabia put her arms around him and kissed him passionately on the lips. He embraced her and returned her kiss.

After a few moments of kissing and holding each other so close that they could hardy breathe, Fabia suddenly broke loose and stood up. She extended her hand and he put her hand in his. He stared into her beautiful eyes. She slowly turned without saying a word and led him to her bedroom.

The next morning, they awoke entwined in each other's arms.

Robert kissed her on the cheek and she pulled him close again. When they finally parted, he said, "I'm going to make breakfast for you, my love. What would you like to eat?"

"I think that I would like some bread and cheese."

"Bread and cheese it will be, my lady. And I, your servant, shall serve you breakfast in bed."

They both laughed uncontrollably. After regaining some of his composure, Robert went to the kitchen and got the bread, cheese, and a small jug of wine.

After breakfast, she said, "Let's spend the time we have left here with each other—instead of going to the Feast of Vulcan."

Robert pulled her close and whispered, "I wish that this morning could last forever, my love."

Around noon, Fabia started to get dressed. "Stay in bed, Marcus." She packed her small bag and knelt by the bedside.

Robert pulled her close and they started kissing again. "I wish that we could stay together forever."

Tears filled her eyes. "So do I, my love, but right now, it seems impossible. Maybe somehow—someday—we will meet again."

"If there is a way, I will find it," he said. "Maybe my father can have your betrothal broken, and we can be together." Secretly he thought that maybe he could ask the Keeper if he could do something to help them. He knew that he would live in Ancient Rome—just to be with Fabia—if he could.

She stood up and said, "Please don't try to follow me. Stay here until you are sure that I am gone." She walked out of the bedroom, carrying her small bag over her shoulder.

Robert heard the front door close. After what seemed an eternity, he sadly got dressed as the full impact of knowing that he may never see her again finally settled in.

He took the control unit for the transporter out of his bag and put the silver chain around his neck. He put the bag over his shoulder and slowly walked out of the house. He locked the door and placed the key behind the loose stone, knowing that Antonius and Livia would never come back to retrieve it.

He was depressed as he slowly walked outside of the city and up the hill to the spot where he had arrived in the transporter. When he was close to the wooded area, he pushed the unlock button on the control unit. Instantly the transporter appeared in front of him with the hydraulic door wide open. He pushed the lock button on the control unit and the hydraulic door closed behind him.

After Robert changed into his twenty-first century clothing, he walked over to the control panel and pushed the lever to the return position. The transporter started to hum again and seemed to lift slightly off of the ground. When the humming stopped and the transporter settled on the ground, the green exit light on the panel started to flash. He pushed the unlock button on his control unit and, when the hydraulic door opened, he was looking at the Never-Ending Road.

He got in his car and sat for a long time. He leaned on the steering wheel with his head buried in his hands. He was thinking of Fabia and how he would try to persuade the Keeper to let him return so that he could be with her.

When Robert was ready to drive back to the Keeper's house, he saw a car parked on the shoulder of the road about twenty-five feet in front of him. The hood on the engine compartment was up and someone was sitting in the driver's seat. He got out and walked up to the driver's side of the other vehicle. A woman with long blonde hair was sitting in the seat with her head buried in her hands. She was weeping.

Robert asked, "Can I help you?"

"No one can help me! I've just lost the only man that I will ever love, and now my car won't start so that I can leave this stupid road. I wish that I had never taken this vacation!"

Robert recognized the voice. Almost immediately, he shouted, "Fabia!"

She removed her hands from her tear-stained face, lifted her head, and looked at him. She was so surprised to see him that she sprung from the car. She almost knocked him over when she tried to leap into his arms and smother him with passionate kisses. They entwined in such a passionate embrace that they could hardly breathe.

As they slowly wound down from their excitement about meeting on the Never-Ending Road, Robert said, "I was going to ask the Keeper to let me live in Rome with you."

"I'm glad that you didn't. You would have never found me. I'm a twenty-first century woman and my real name is Jennifer Haines."

"My name isn't Marcus. It's Robert Wright—and I'm also from the twenty-first century. We have to talk."

He took Jennifer by the hand and walked to a bench at the side of the road where they could sit and talk. Jennifer was a nurse, working in a hospital not far from his school. She had never been able to find the man of her dreams and was content to end up as an old maid—until she received the letter from the Keeper. She thought that she might take a vacation on some exotic island and meet someone and she accepted the invitation to travel on the Never-Ending Road.

When she started driving, she saw the sign for Pompeii. She had read about the city and thought that she would take a brief visit and then find her exotic island. As she was walking, she met Livia. Livia thought that she had come from Rome to visit. Livia took her home and introduced her to her uncle. They both welcomed her as part of the family.

Jennifer said that she was thinking about telling them that she could only stay until the next day, but when they were walking out of the garden, Antonius introduced her to an incredibly handsome young man named Marcus Valerius—and she decided to stay.

Robert kissed her. "I'm glad that you decided to stay in Pompeii."

"So am I."

They locked in a passionate embrace and kissed until Jennifer broke loose and asked, "Do you think that the Keeper of the Never-Ending Road is some kind of a matchmaker?"

"You know I was thinking about that myself. Why don't we go and ask him?"

"That's a good idea. But can you try to start my car first?"

"All right," answered Robert. He looked under the hood, but didn't notice anything visibly wrong. He told Jennifer to try to start the car again.

She turned the key and the engine started instantly. "That's strange. I tried to start my car dozens of times before you arrived—and there wasn't even a sound of the engine trying to crank over. Do you think that the Keeper had anything to do with it?"

"I wouldn't be surprised. Push the red button on your control unit and drive down the Never-Ending Road. I'll follow you in my car. The road should lead us back to the Keeper's house. When we drop off our control units, we can ask the Keeper all of our questions. I'm sure that he can answer them. I know that I have quite a few."

"So do I."

Robert got in his car and followed her down the Never-Ending road to the Keeper's house. When they pulled up the driveway, they got out of their cars and walked up to the door. The brown wooden basket was on the step next to the door. Robert rang the doorbell and they waited for several minutes. When no one answered, he started knocking, but no one answered. They walked around to the rear of the building to see if the Keeper was on the patio or in the garden. The Keeper of the Never-Ending Road was nowhere to be found. When they walked around to the front door, Robert rang the doorbell again.

Jennifer looked down and there was an envelope taped onto the handle of the basket. On the envelope was written: Robert and Jennifer. Jennifer removed the envelope and said, "I didn't see that envelope when we walked up to the house."

"I don't remember seeing one either."

She opened the envelope and removed a handwritten note. She read it out loud.

Dear Robert and Jennifer:

I'm sorry that I couldn't be here when you finished your vacation. I had an emergency and won't return for several days. I hope that both of you had a pleasant vacation. Please leave your control units in the basket.

Thank you,
The Keeper of the Never-Ending Road

Robert looked at Jennifer and said, "I think that the Keeper doesn't want us to ask him any questions, and if we come back a month from now he won't answer his door. I'm sure that he planned everything and that our meeting was not a coincidence."

"Maybe the Keeper is some kind of a matchmaker."

They smiled at each other and tossed their control units into the basket. When they got back to their cars, they exchanged phone numbers and addresses. They got in their cars and Robert followed Jennifer home to make sure that she arrived safely.

"They are going to be married next August and eventually have two children that will look just like Silvanus and Junia. They will name their children Brad and Hanna. I'll bet you are wondering how I know all of these things. Well, I know because I am the Keeper of the Never-Ending Road.

Make sure that you check all of your mail, because one day you may receive an envelope with a gold border around the edges. Don't mistake it for junk mail. Read it! You may find that you have just been invited to a free, all-expense paid vacation on my Never-Ending Road."

***

ABOUT THE AUTHOR

Earle W. Hanna Sr. has been writing for pleasure since he was fifteen, when his first short story was published. He was inspired to continue writing as a student at Temple University in Philadelphia. He lives in Langhorne, Pennsylvania, and is a member of the National Writers Association.

CPSIA information can be obtained at www.ICGtesting.com
Printed in the USA
LVOW08s1926010414
379875LV00002B/178/P